THE CAIAPHAS CODE

An ALEX HUNT Adventure Thriller

URCELIA TEIXEIRA

SPECIAL THANKS

Special Thanks

To those who have lost a loved one to the
current worldwide pandemic,
may you find peace in your sadness and
may God be with you in your time of sorrow.
You are in my thoughts and prayers.

JOIN THE ADVENTURE

R eceive a **FREE** copy of the prequel and see where it all started!

NOT AVAILABLE IN STORES!

Click on image or enter http://download.urcelia.com in your browser

PREFACE

On Friday, April 3, AD 33 a high priest filled with jealousy and rage, cunningly plotted the torturous public killing of an innocent man. The man's unjust death was vindicated by the very power they had said he sacrilegiously acted against.

Put to shame and shunned by the people and his once revered Roman followers, the high priest fled to a neighboring country where he eventually died in AD 46. It is said he was tormented with guilt and self-loathing until he drew his very last breath. But before he died, in a final desperate attempt for forgiveness, hoping for his soul to be set free, he hid the two souvenirs he had secretly kept in repentance of what he had done.

His name was Caiaphas and his penitent keepsakes are about to be found.

PROLOGUE

AD 33, JERUSALEM

L oud rumblings echoed from the riots in the streets outside the stately palace, forcing Caiaphas, the Jewish high priest, to his feet. From his opulent courtyard balcony he stared at the people in the street down below.

"What's happening down there?" he asked one of his elders who went by the name Nicodemus.

"We might have another protest on our hands, High Priest. It seems they're accusing the Roman State of using temple funds to build the aqueduct. Hundreds are heading to Pilate to complain as we speak."

"That must not happen! We need to stop them before they can get anywhere near him."

"I'll take care of it, High Priest," the head of his guard jumped to command behind him.

Nicodemus paused, nervously tugging at his gray beard. "We might have a bigger problem on our hands."

"Bigger than a rebellion?" Caiaphas sneered.

Nicodemus stopped, forcing Caiaphas to turn and face him.

"There's a man from Galilee... a Jew. The priests reported that he turned over the collection tables in the temple."

"Yes, I heard. It seems he's causing quite a stir amongst the people."

"Yes, well, it's gotten worse. The people are turning away from the temple and choosing to follow him instead. He's performing miracles all over Jerusalem."

"Sorcery is what I call it," a second elder, who stood to the high priest's right added. "He's put a spell on the people. They're mesmerized by his wonders."

Caiaphas turned and walked back into his house. "And? He's not the first to trick people into seeing things. They'll be back in our temple soon enough."

"I'm not so sure. He's different, High Priest. The people seem to be clinging to his every word. They like him and much of what he says is like that of a prophet. From what I hear he speaks words of wisdom," Nicodemus replied.

"Careful, Nicodemus. Need I remind you where your loyalties lie?"

Nicodemus ignored the insinuation and continued his report without arguing. "The people are refusing to pay their temple taxes since they're not attending our sermons anymore."

Caiaphas stopped dead in his tracks. The last report had got his attention.

"How many people are we talking about?"

"Hundreds, High Priest, gaining more with each passing day," a second elder answered.

"Well we can't let that happen, can we? If he continues turning the people away from the temple the treasury will run dry and we will lose all of this." Caiaphas gestured to the luxurious surroundings in his home. "Not to mention Pilate will have us all flogged," he continued, and then paused in front of his copper basin signaling to one of his servants to run water over his hands.

"Assemble the chief priests and the other elders immediately," he instructed both elders.

When darkness had fallen and a small group of his chief priests had gathered behind closed doors in his palace, the riots had all but quieted down in the village streets.

"What do you know of this man who threatens to destroy our temple?" Caiaphas asked them. "Have any of you witnessed his sacrilege against the house of God?"

No one answered him. The high priest paused briefly in front of each of the eight members, hoping his stern eyes would encourage them to speak up, but still no one spoke.

"We need to stop him," Caiaphas continued. "We cannot have him go around tricking the Romans and calling himself the Messiah, king of the Jews. I will not have this man challenge my authority and corrupt the people against this house with his blasphemy, especially during Passover."

Low murmurs erupted among the priests as the gravity of their leader's last statement suddenly dawned on them and one of them commented in panic.

"We're expecting thousands for Passover, High Priest. If they all follow this man we'd have no one to charge at the *mikvehs*." (The chief priest was referring to the ritual immersion baths required by Jewish law upon entering the temple.)

Caiaphas knew all too well this surcharge yielded the most profit, especially during a sizable annual event like Passover. The threat of lost income angered him and when the rest of the group slowly caught on to what might come from it, it set about an uproar amongst the group of riled men.

"We need to remove him before he destroys everything we stand for," the high priest guided his holy order.

"Remove him? What do you mean?" Nicodemus, who had been observing quietly, questioned his leader.

"You heard me. He needs to be executed. It's the only way," Caiaphas responded.

"Crucifixion, High Priest! He's not a murderous thief. Surely you do not have the authority to sentence an innocent man to death for mere intimidation. None of us has even witnessed his supposed blasphemy. There has to be another way," Nicodemus challenged his superior.

Caiaphas turned and faced his elder. "I have ruled this supreme house for eighteen years because I stay true to our cause. I would suggest you do the same. Bring him to me and find three witnesses who will testify to his treason and blasphemy. I will present their testimonies to Pilate and he will no doubt support my cause. Now leave me in peace and find me my witnesses. We have to be quick about this before the Passover starts."

Several members of the Sanhedrin agreed with their supreme leader, except for Nicodemus who silently turned and walked towards the exit.

"Nicodemus," Caiaphas called after his elder, "You know nothing at all! You do not realize that it is better for you that one man die for the people than that the whole nation perish."

. . .

Before the light of the new day, a man by the name of Judas, who was reportedly one of the man's closest friends, was paid thirty pieces of silver to lead the Roman soldiers to the wanted man. Arrested and thrown into the dungeon prison chambers beneath Caiaphas' home, the man from Galilee silently awaited his accusers.

"We have done as you asked, High Priest. The man has been captured," Nicodemus reported.

"And the witnesses?"

"None of their accounts correspond, High Priest. We're going to have to let him go."

"That's not going to happen, Nicodemus. Have you tried rewarding them?"

Nicodemus shifted his weight uncomfortably.

"That would be deceitful, High Priest."

He paused, realizing he'd need to approach his superior from a different angle if he were to be successful at setting the innocent man free. "If the people find out you falsified testimony they would not look kindly upon your actions, High Priest. It is best for this house to set the man free."

But Nicodemus' words did not penetrate the hardened heart of his high priest and Caiaphas continued.

"Then we will trick him into confessing that he is the Messiah in front of us all so we can stand witness ourselves. Assemble the Sanhedrin at once. Before the sun sets, if it's the last thing I do, this man will be brought before Pilate and crucified for all the people to witness."

CHAPTER 1

CURRENT DAY, JERUSALEM

I t wasn't until that moment that Luke realized his life was in grave danger. With his heart pulsing in his ears his feet descended the closed stairwell in his hostel three steps at a time as he ran to escape whoever was now chasing after him. The horrific images of his best friend's brutal killing mere moments ago flashed through his mind that now raced at a million miles an hour. If he had any chance of staying alive he'd have to try and get to the Old City. It was the closest public place he could think of right now.

With his mind fixed on getting out of the building he hardly registered the sickening panic that threatened to exit through his mouth. He'd have to keep it together and stay focused, he silently reminded himself again. Mere moments later he heard the stairwell door open three floors above him, soon followed by thumping footsteps down towards him. He jumped the last four steps onto the landing and narrowly escaped a single bullet that ricocheted off the wall just above his left ear. Adrenaline thrust his body faster down the last flight of stairs while he kept his eyes pinned on the door of the humble building's fire escape in front of him. He yanked the crossbar lever down and pushed both his flat palms against the hard metal before he welcomed the warm late afternoon sun on his face.

The graffitied street behind the hostel was quiet, lined only with several stationary cars trailing the narrow road in both directions. His mind ordered him to turn left in the direction of the Old City and he didn't hesitate. He dared not stop and waste even one second. With his eyes focused on where he'd need to turn the corner up ahead he listened out for the hostel's exit door behind him and when he didn't detect any sound coming from it, found relief knowing they hadn't caught up with him yet. The steel-gray scribbled walls soon blended into sand colored limestone walls that suggested he was getting closer to his destination, and moments later he turned up into the bustling street that led to the Jaffa Gate. His eyes frantically searched for signs of an ambush. He'd have to be prepared for anything. There was no telling how many of them were after him.

Cars and buses coming from both directions made it harder for him to cross the busy double lane road to where the familiar Old City walls beckoned up ahead. Deciding to chance it he ran into the traffic, only just avoiding an oncoming tour bus followed by a taxi and two more cars. Having now reached the narrow pedestrian island between the opposite lanes, he again chanced the oncoming traffic but wasn't so lucky this time round. His body thudded on top of a car's hood before it bounced off and slammed onto the hard sidewalk. With no time to ponder any injuries, he jumped to his feet and raced toward the stone portal in Jerusalem's historic Old City walls. He took a few seconds and turned to look behind him for the first time as he entered through the arched entrance. In the distance he spotted three men causing a commotion in the street where he nearly got killed by the car and he hurried his escape between the crowds that were making their way through the entrance into the ancient city. Inside the Old City's stone walls he picked up his pace and ran toward the congested market stalls that wound their way through the narrow cobbled streets. Careful not to announce his position by causing a distur-bance he stealthily forged on while his mind raced for a way out from their pursuit. He knew they would be close on his heels but didn't care to verify his suspicions at this stage. All he needed to do was focus on disappearing... and fast.

He briefly ran his hand over his hip that suddenly emitted sharp pangs of pain down his leg where it had collided with the vehicle. I can't slow down now, the silent warning echoed in his mind.

A small group of Muslim women scattered when he interrupted their afternoon gathering in front of a spice vendor and Luke quickly changed direction to throw his pursuers off his trail. He was heading toward the Jewish Quarter as far as he could tell. He and Nathan had only been in Jerusalem three weeks so he wasn't yet fully familiar with the location. But what he did recall from their guided tour mere weeks ago was that the Old City was divided into four residential quarters and when the Islamic residents gradually lessened and the number of Jewish men and women increased, it confirmed his assumption had paid off. It was a smart move on his part since he was confident his pursuers weren't Jewish which meant they'd certainly raise a few eyebrows if found running through the Jewish Quarter.

Surrounded by teenage students who studied at the nearby *yeshivas*, Luke decided to slow his pace to a brisk walk instead. It was too crowded for him to comfortably continue running and he desperately needed to catch his breath and rest his injured hip. Besides, he was convinced he had managed to shake his hunters. His nostrils filled with the most delicious aroma of freshly baked bagels and he was suddenly reminded of home back in Canberra, Australia. In a moment of weakness he cursed his father for insisting he join Nathan in tracing their Jewish roots. He'd far rather have spent his time soaking up the sun on Bondi beach like all the other college students did during spring break. Now Nathan had been killed and he might be next. Panic flushed his veins making him pick up his pace again. The narrow alleyways through the Jewish precinct eventually met up to the Western Wall where the low murmurs of praying Jews provided him with some form of comfort. He paused in the middle of the open public square, carefully turning three hundred and sixty degrees to detect if he was still in any danger. Surrounded by tourists and people from all three of the practicing religions, he took in the divided but harmonious worship of Jews praying at the Western Wall, Muslims kneeling, facing south, and the Christians worshiping by singing praise behind him. All within the same city walls but distinctly opposing each other's beliefs.

From the corner of his eye he spotted a ruckus amongst the crowds of onlookers on the outer edges of the sizable public gathering place and realized he was dangerously close to being discovered. If he ran now he'd alert them to his position, so he did the only thing that was left to do and, with his head turned downward, slowly but steadily moved in the opposite direction. Behind the infamous Wailing Wall the impressive gold dome on Temple Mount glistened in the last rays of the sun. Hiding on the mount wasn't an option; they'd be closing the entrance soon. Getting there would also mean he'd have to follow the overhead walkway and risk being seen for certain. His eyes searched for another way out and he spotted one of the other entrance gates into the city. He had no idea where it would lead him but it proved his only option; he was trapped otherwise. Without hesitation he increased his pace and headed in the direction of the Dung Gate. But there was no escaping his friend's killers and they soon spotted him. Luke's steady pace increased to a light jog and he silently prayed he wouldn't be stopped and questioned by security. His prayers were answered and he soon managed to successfully exit the Old City. Hordes of tourists were getting into their parked tour buses making it easier for Luke to disappear between them, but the men had already seen him exit through the gate. On a slight downward slope, the narrow road along the city wall snaked away from the historic Old City. His trainers slammed down hard and fast onto the asphalt. As the people became fewer the further he ran, so too did the traffic and before long Luke found himself in altogether unfamiliar desolate territory. The sun had just about set completely, and being out from under the harsh lights of the historic tourist venue and cars, made it much harder for him to find his way. But he kept running. As long as it was away from them.

Low limestone walls atop which the one closest to him included a high barbwire fence, flanked the road. On the other side of the fence, in the dusk light, he could just about make out a slight slope leading down the hill toward what looked like ruins or a deserted village under construction. When the fence a few feet further on offered a gaping hole, he grabbed the opportunity and squeezed his body through it. Suddenly on uneven rocky soil he lost his footing and tumbled down the hilltop. His already bruised hip shot new bolts of pain through his body as it hit the sharp edges of several large rocks on his way down the mound. Prickly bushes and thorny broken off branches scratched his hands and the bottom part of his legs as he reached out in an attempt to slow down, but it was only when his body thumped hard against a jagged boulder that it stopped the out-of-control motion of his body.

Hidden behind the large rock wall on the outskirts of Jerusalem, Luke rested his head back against the rugged dusty object and briefly cast his eyes at the full moon above his head. If ever there was a night he despised it being a full moon it was tonight. Conscious of the fact that his hiding place wasn't obscure enough, he pulled his knees to his chest, making himself as invisible as possible. With any luck his fall had aided his escape and he could rest there for a bit until the coast was clear, he thought, hoping he had run fast enough to begin with.

A light breeze blew a fresh mist of orange desert dust in his face that stuck to his sweaty skin. He wiped his face on his sleeve, instantly regretting it when instead it made it worse and left a layer of gritty dirt scraping over his fresh scratches where the bushes had caught him. It was well past midnight and he and Nathan had been on the run for two days already. Had he known it was going to turn out like this he would have never taken it. His hand reached into his pants pocket where his fingers traced the small hard item he had put there after they killed Nathan. If only he had listened to Nathan none of this would have happened and his friend would still be alive. He shut his eyes in a futile attempt to stop the tears from escaping down his clammy cheeks as he recalled the events a mere forty eight hours ago.

"Luke you're crazy! What if someone catches us?" Nathan had warned him.

"Oh come on Nate, where's your sense of adventure? No one will see us. We didn't give up Bondi so we could be stuck here with a bunch of geriatrics and a boring tour guide. We'll be back before they miss us," he had stupidly replied.

Nathan had always been the sensible one between them, always following the rules, never straying too far from the law. Luke, on the other hand, pushed the envelope in pretty much anything and everything he did in life. No matter how hard he tried he'd always find himself—and anyone with him—in some kind of a mess, as if trouble always found him. And now here he was, alone and desperately afraid for his life with no one coming to his rescue while his best friend was dead... all because of him.

CHAPTER 2

When the loud noise of a distant construction vehicle jerked Luke to consciousness, he realized he must have fallen asleep. As reality settled in he held his position for a brief moment. Still lying curled up in the dirt at the foot of the arid rocky mound, hidden behind the boulder that had saved his life the night before, he listened intently. Apart from a dog barking in the distance, and the drumming noise of the construction vehicle somewhere to his right, it seemed quiet. He slowly shifted his weight onto his elbow and raised his head, instantly flinching with pain as his palm pushed down onto a thorn that was attached to a broken-off piece of foliage next to him. The gray three-inch needlelike thorn instantly drew blood where it had pushed half an inch into his flesh and now left a sharp sting behind when he pulled it out. Momentarily distracted by the incident he cautiously pulled himself into a hunched position behind the boulder. His eyes searched the terrain around him and settled on the gold dome that lay a fair distance away. He hadn't realized he'd run as far as he had the night before. Completely removed from the bustling streets surrounding the Old City, Luke rose to his feet somewhere on the outskirts of Jerusalem. He had rolled halfway down a steep slope to where he now found himself on the edge of a large construction site.

His body was stiff and bruised and his lips were dry. In an attempt to wet it with his tongue he tasted the chalky tang of caked soil where it had settled on his sweaty face during the night. Above his head the sun was already hot. He had no idea what time it was and since he had never really showed any interest in survival techniques he didn't have a clue about how to use the sun as a guide either. What he did know was that he had somehow managed to escape death. For how long, he couldn't be sure.

He managed to gather a small amount of saliva and spat it on the inside of the hem of his once pale blue shirt before wiping his eyes, repeating the process until he no longer had any spit left. In that moment he had never felt more alone. In their haste to get away and out from under the surprise attack that had left his childhood friend dead the night before, he had also left his passport behind at the hostel; the very reason they had gone back there. If he went back for it a second time they might very well be waiting for him again. A wave of emotion rippled through his aching body. He knew he couldn't bear the sight of seeing his friend's body anyway. His mind searched through the days of the week and realized they weren't booked in on any tours for another three days. As it stood, no one would miss either of them until at least then. He turned and looked back down the hill to where the construction workers were oblivious to his presence, and pondered whether he should chance asking them for help. How, he wouldn't know. He didn't speak either Hebrew or Arabic and chances were they'd give him the once-over and realize they'd have to report him. What's more, he knew nothing about his attackers. For all he was aware they'd have eyes and ears everywhere. Heck, they might even be law enforcement. He'd heard many stories about how the law wasn't always principled in these countries. After all, he had taken something that didn't belong to him.

Deciding he'd lay low for another day before attempting to find his way to the Australian Embassy, he slowly started crawling back up the hill, every so often inspecting his surrounds. When he reached the top where it met up with a narrow road, he climbed over the low wall, held his head down and cautiously set off along the road away from the city. In a ridiculous attempt to make himself invisible, he stuck his hands inside the pockets of his jeans but came to a sudden standstill when his fingertips brushed over the small, hard object he had momentarily forgotten was there. He paused, turning to see if anyone was around to see him before he pulled the item from his pocket. In the harsh morning sunlight the ancient piece of loot glistened where the grime had rubbed off and he found himself staring curiously at it. He'd known it had to be worth something when he found it in that forest, but enough to kill over, that surprised him. He rolled it between his fingers, squinting as the sun's rays reflected off the top. How did they even know he had found it? Apart from Nathan, no one else knew they had strayed to the forest, much less that he had picked up an ancient artifact. Sudden doubt about Nathan's loyalty caught him by surprise and he instantly regretted even considering it. Feeling as if he had just betrayed his friend he fought back the guilt. He had been friends with Nathan long enough to know he would have never told a soul. Regret welled up inside and he contemplated tossing the item down the hill, but then changed his mind. If he did manage to safely get to the embassy he'd need to prove why they'd killed Nathan.

Conscious of the fact that he had been rooted to the spot for too long, he shoved the silver object back into his pocket, glancing over his shoulder to see if he was still alone before he continued down the winding road. Moments later the low murmuring sound of a vehicle's engine whirred behind him. He tucked his head into his chest as it slowly rolled down the hill towards him. His heart pounded hard and fast against his ribs as he prayed the car would pass him by. Thankfully, it did, and he found himself inconspicuously glancing up at it as it drove past. The dusty red car was occupied by a man old enough to be his grandfather, a local it seemed, who had seen it all before and who could not care less about a scruffy foreigner walking along a quiet road. As the sun's rays beat down harder, Luke found himself silently counting out his footsteps, each time stopping at three before starting over, as if he was rehearsing the waltz. He willed his mind away from the memories of how his mother had taught him the waltz before his homecoming. He dared not allow his mind to meditate on whether he'd ever see his parents again. Instead, he pinned his eyes on where, up ahead, the road made a sharp turn to the left and wound around a steep embankment. As he turned the corner his eyes settled on what appeared to be ruins of some kind at the foot of the slope. Nestled in the shade of several lush green trees and surrounded by equally verdant bushes it appeared almost oasis-like, in direct contrast to its desert-like surroundings. The thought crossed his mind that he was imagining it and he pinched his eyes open and shut a few times. But it wasn't a mirage. It was very real. Excited about the prospect that there could very well be a small source of water and that he might be able to hide out there, he set off down the side of the mound towards it, letting his body slide down in places where the soil beneath his feet was loose. When he reached the green patch he paused in the shade of a tree that now seemed much larger than had been apparent from the road. His eyes carefully traced over the stone remains of the ancient structure in the middle of nowhere. Relieved to find it wasn't a tourist site as was fairly common anywhere around Jerusalem, he carefully started walking around it before eventually stepping over a pile of slabs that led down into a square sunken area. The ruin wasn't very big and oddly divided into several strange smaller square basins leading away from where he stood against the slope. If he weren't as tired and clearly in the process of losing his sanity, he'd have thought they were small shallow stone swimming pools. He caught himself smiling. If Nathan were there, he'd have known exactly what it was, he thought.

From the corner of his eye he caught sight of a ripe fig hanging from the low branches of the nearby tree.

"No way!" he exclaimed out loud and leaped to snatch it off. Barely a second later he had peeled and shoved it in his mouth, allowing the sweet juice to trickle down his dirty chin. He tossed what was left of the fruit stuck to its peel before plucking several more, balancing them on his forearm against his chest before he sat down in the shade of the large tree. When his tummy eventually pushed firmly against the button of his jeans, he stopped and wiped his hands across his pants in an attempt to get the fig tree's sticky, white, milky liquid off his fingers. But it only made it worse. As he took a moment to rest, his eyes trailed the sunken squares and settled on the furthest one that stopped slightly higher than the rest under another tree. When he laid eyes on the bright green grass around it he jumped to his feet and rushed over.

"Please, please let there be water," he prayed out loud.

When he jumped the final empty recessed basin, the hot sun's rays shimmered off the welcoming liquid that trickled from an underground tube protruding from the embankment above the concavity. Not sparing a moment he threw his body into the hollow space taking up position below the pipe and allowed the slow flowing crisp, clean water to run over his face and eventually into his mouth. Loud giggles escaped Luke's exhausted body between gulping down several cupped hands of water. When he had finally had his fill and got most of the grime off his face and body, he settled under the tree and closed his eyes for a brief moment.

And as he lay there in his moment of joy he fell into a deep sleep. So deep that he never heard them coming.

CHAPTER 3

M att Taylor tucked his face into his elbow in an attempt to cover his mouth and nose.

"It never gets easier, does it, Ronita?" he said to his colleague where they stood paused over the corpse on the floor. His eyes glanced around the small modest but functional hostel room where a local forensics team was already busy processing the scene. Next to him his female colleague's fingers enthusiastically tapped the screen of her iPad. Ronita Bhambri was a highly skilled team member and they worked well together. She also knew her boss well enough by now to know he wasn't expecting her to answer.

"What have they given us to work with?" Matt asked her.

"The victim's name was Nathan Levi, aged twenty-two, a PhD student at ANU. They're still trying to locate his parents. Apparently they're on a cruise ship somewhere," Ronita informed him.

Matt snapped one black silicone glove over his right hand and lowered himself next to the body, careful not to disturb the crime scene. Ronita leaned in next to him and watched as Matt pulled away a bloodstained sleeve to reveal the vague marking on Nathan's left forearm. Rigor had already set in which made it harder to twist the student's arm in order to fully expose the image.

"Don't touch him," an assertive male voice approached them from behind.

Matt straightened up and turned to lay eyes on an Israeli man who quickly proceeded to bark instructions in Hebrew at the forensics team that was scattered throughout the small room; visibly upset because they had invited Matt and Ronita onto his crime scene.

Matt pulled the rubber glove off and held his hand out to introduce himself.

"You must be Ravid. Matt Taylor from—"

"Spare me the introduction, Agent Taylor. I know who you are and I don't like that you're here."

"Wow, you don't mince your words, do you?" Matt said, amused.

"Let's get one thing straight, Taylor. You're only here because my orders came from the prime minister. This is still my crime scene and if you think you're going to tango in here and take over you've got another thing coming."

Ronita buried her face in her iPad when Matt's obvious amusement was hard to miss. Although their work was demanding and required them to take things seriously, her boss had a great sense of humor, the one thing that often got them through the more unpleasant aspects of their job.

"Good, because I don't intend on doing your job for you, Ravid. Homicide isn't part of my repertoire. I'm only interested in the imprint on your victim's arm," Matt responded, "and I think you mean waltz, not tango."

The Israeli detective wasn't used to being told off, much less on his own turf. That was quite evident when his tanned olive skin blazed into a light shade of pink that left his flaring nostrils white around the edges.

"Well?" Matt sarcastically beckoned to the corpse on the floor. "Are you going to show me what I came here for so I can get out of your way?"

Ravid's dark eyes said it all but he chose not to speak. Instead he hollered instructions at a timid looking colleague behind him who promptly handed over a brown document case.

"That's everything you need, Taylor. I expect you to share anything you might discover on your own in return. Now if you don't mind, I have a murderer to catch."

Matt had already scanned though the contents of the file.

"Actually, I'll need a copy of the post-mortem examination report when that's done, please. I'm hoping your pathologist can give us more information about the image."

"Yes, well that might take a while. We're still trying to locate his parents who'd need to consent to us doing the autopsy. For now you'll have to make do with what's in there." Ravid turned and disappeared between his men leaving his assistant to usher Matt and Ronita from the room.

"Is your boss always this grumpy?" Matt asked the quiet assistant.

"He takes his work very seriously, Agent Taylor, and when he thinks his hand was forced and people might step on his toes, he gets a bit defensive. We don't often have Australian students murdered in our city."

"Well I don't intend on stepping on anyone's toes, I assure you. I'm just here about that image on his arm and how it connects to this poor guy getting murdered. The *who* is for you guys to figure out."

"Good day, Agent Taylor. Let me know if there's anything else you need from us," the assistant politely replied before joining Ravid inside the hostel room.

. . .

A t their makeshift headquarters in a nearby hotel, Matt flung his denim jacket onto the sofa before he took up a standing position near the window.

"Back so soon?" A young man who was seated in the corner jumped up from behind three computer screens.

"Not out of choice, I assure you," Ronita answered. "Local law enforcement didn't exactly welcome our presence." She handed him a few pages from the document folder.

Matt, who was deep in thought where he still stood staring out the window spoke. "All right then, team, we have our work cut out for us on this one. Working a murder isn't exactly part of our expertise and it's clear we're not going to get much help from Ravid so let's figure this thing out ourselves. Red, see if you can pick up any pictures of the victim on social media. He was a student and they usually love posting pictures of themselves. Check flight schedules, tour packages, the works. I saw another toothbrush in the bathroom; he wasn't here on his own. Find out who he was with, and see if you can pick up any camera footage off the surveillance cameras anywhere in the city."

The computer geek known only as Red due to his bright red hair and freckled face didn't hesitate and moments later the clickety-clack sounds from his keyboard sounded throughout the room.

Matt moved over to where Ronita had sat down on the couch and spread a series of photos across the stone coffee table in front of them, paying particular interest to the one that showed the victim's arm.

"Okay, let's see what we have here," Matt said as his eyes moved between the photos. "Let's just play devil's advocate here for the moment and assume they're wrong about it being an ancient religious imprint of some kind. We need to exclude any other possible theories first," Matt suggested while moving the photos around on the table before continuing. "It's on his right arm. Judging from the callus on his middle finger he was right-handed so it's not something he wrote on his arm and then washed off. It's not a tattoo either."

"Perhaps a stamp from a night club?" Ronita ventured.

"Possible but I doubt it. I managed to have a fairly decent look at it before Ravid arrived and it didn't look like temporary ink markings of any kind. Besides, most nightclubs use invisible ink these days and let's not forget we're in Jerusalem. I doubt the nightclubs here are that sophisticated or even have the need for access control." Matt got up and walked around to the back of the sofa where he ran his hand through his mousy brown hair before placing both elbows on the backrest.

"It also doesn't help that these photos are out of focus. Would it have killed the man to let us have a better look and take our own? It's hard to tell for sure what we're looking at from these images. We might have no option now but to wait for that autopsy report," Matt concluded.

"Smart kid to have left us a clue though, right?" Red commented while his fingers continued striking the keys.

"Who says he left a clue? It could just as well be evidence left behind by the killer," Ronita argued.

"Okay, kids, let's trace back. Red, what have you found so far?" Matt asked.

"Well, he was smart, I will tell you that. He was top of his class at the Australian National University. Looks like he had a head for numbers and stats. He arrived at Ben Gurion Airport two weeks ago accompanied by another student, Luke Cohen, a philosophy student also at ANU. I found their school yearbook and it appears they've been friends for most of their schooldays. They have a return ticket booked back to Canberra three weeks from now. They're both Jewish and came here on tourist visas. They've done several local tourist attractions through a local tour company and were due to travel down to the Dead Sea where they were meant to have booked in at a local B & B two days ago. The hostel super discovered the body when he went in to clean the room. Other than that I can't find any irregular activities that might indicate he was involved with anything illegal."

"Good work. See if you can pick anything up on this Luke kid's whereabouts. Check the street cameras behind the hostel, credit card activity, local ATMs anything. He might still be alive and know something," Matt said.

"You're assuming he's in danger. You don't think it's possible that he might have killed Nathan? Perhaps they had an argument and things got out of hand. Guys his age always fight over girls," Ronita theorized.

"How would you know?" Red teased her.

"Just because I come from a traditional Indian family doesn't mean I don't know how immature men can be," she bit back.

Matt moved back to the window and stared out across Jerusalem, ignoring the childish squabble between his younger team members. From where they were on the eighth floor he could see the entire Jordan valley and the Dead Sea in the far distance. His mind mulled over the information, Ronita's theory, and the details he recalled from their brief visit to the crime scene. He tried not to think about the tragedy that had befallen this young man. That only made their job harder. Ronita was right, the two friends could have argued about something.

"Well, this is interesting," Ronita commented from where her fingers moved over the trackpad on her laptop.

"What?" Matt moved in behind her and watched as she held up the photo of the imprint next to her screen.

"I thought I'd pull up some images on early religious symbols, just in case, and this one seems to match the pattern almost perfectly."

"What are we looking at?" Matt asked as he angled his head.

"It's an ancient seal used on a scroll that was discovered in a cave in the Jordan Valley and dates back to around AD 40. See this chainlike pattern here? It's identical." Ronita's pointed finger moved between the two images.

"Can you find more information on it?" Matt prompted.

"No, that's all. There's not a lot about anything dating back this far in biblical history, nothing on the Internet, at least. I can call up the museum where the scroll is kept and see if perhaps they'll let us see it."

Matt nodded, giving Ronita the go ahead.

"Matt, I have cameras in the Old City that caught Luke running through the Jewish Quarter on his own but no sight of Nathan. Luke entered through the Jaffa Gate and left soon after through the Dung Gate. Timestamps indicate he must have been running since it was quite a lot of ground to cover in such a short amount of time. This was about three days ago."

"So he was chased," Matt stated.

"I'd say so, yes," Red confirmed.

"Excellent work, Red. Anything after he left the Old City?"

"Nothing. There's one camera right outside the gate confirming his exit and then nothing."

"Get in touch with Ravid and see if you can get him to send a few men to search along this road here." He pointed to the road leading away from the gate on Red's computer screen.

Ronita's voice cut across the room.

"The museum says the scroll went missing shortly after it was found. They suspect it was an inside job. This photo was the only evidence proving its discovery and somehow it got leaked on Facebook," she reported.

Matt inspected the two images more closely. He couldn't deny the striking similarity in the patterns. It certainly was the only lead they had and worth at least following up on.

"You said it was discovered in a cave in the Jordan Valley. Any chance you can find out where this cave is?" Matt asked.

"You're not thinking of taking us into a cave, are you?" Ronita said with slight nervousness in her voice.

"Us, no. But I most definitely have someone in mind," Matt declared with a mischievous smile. "Just find me the exact location and any other information you can dig up on the cave and this scroll. Work your magic team and leave the rest to me."

CHAPTER 4

"Well, look what the cat dragged in," Matt said when Alex and Sam entered their hotel headquarters.

"It's nice to see you too, Ollie," Alex greeted him, followed by Sam.

"Ollie? Who's Ollie?" Ronita said puzzled as she stepped up to meet them.

"Just a pet name Sheila has for me," Matt said with a playful tone.

"Sheila? I thought you said her name was Alex?" Ronita responded, more confused than ever.

Matt laughed. "Team, this is *the* Alex Hunt and Dr. Sam Quinn, all the way from England. They're the best in the business. We met years ago in Cambodia... had a little rendezvous with a bear and some rogue mercenaries."

"That's putting it mildly," Sam added. "That place almost killed us. But, what I wouldn't do for a plate of your bear stew." Sam mmmed and licked his lips as if he had taken a mouthful.

"Ah, good times, my friend. So I understand the two of you got hooked. It seems I was right on the nose back then," Matt said with pride.

"She couldn't resist me," Sam teased.

"Well judging from all this there's clearly been some changes in your life too," Alex said as she took in their surroundings. "It's a far cry from your jungle cabin in Cambodia," she continued.

"Really? I hadn't noticed," Matt joked.

"I take it you still work for ASIO," Sam asked.

"They're not going to get rid of me anytime soon. Things get a bit heated every now and then but at least I now have my own team. It's just us three taking on the world. Ronita here is the best field agent there is, and that's our computer genius, Red. Let's just say he literally holds the world at his fingertips with that keyboard of his. And with great allies like the two of you to help every now and then we're invincible," he added with a wink.

"Speaking of which, just what exactly are we getting ourselves into here? You were a bit vague in your message," Alex said from where she now half-sat on the windowsill.

"That's what we're hoping you could help us figure out, to be honest. We don't have a lot to go on as things stand right now," Ronita answered.

Matt beckoned for Alex and Sam to join him at the table and spread out the photographs of Nathan's body.

"This was Nathan, a student from Canberra, here on what seems to have been a holiday. He was found murdered three days ago with this marking on his forearm. The Israeli government suspects religious activity might be related to his killing."

"Satanic?" Sam said in a low tone.

"Not necessarily. More like illegal trade of religious artifacts. There's a lot of smuggling rings operating in this part of the world. Unfortunately, we weren't allowed to examine the corpse up close and we're still waiting on the autopsy report. So this is all we have, a bunch of bad photos taken of the imprint on his arm and a not-so-detailed coroner's report that's supposed to mean something. Ronita managed to come across a leaked image on Facebook of a scroll that was discovered in a cave some time back. The seal on the scroll shows remarkable similarity, but we can't verify it because the scroll was stolen from the museum shortly after it was found. And that's where the two of you come in. If there's a relic to be found, who better to do it than you."

Alex studied the photo of the imprint on the dead student's arm before doing the same with the image Ronita had found of the scroll.

"Well, what do you think?" Matt pushed when Alex remained quiet.

"I think your suspicions are correct. My guess is we're looking at an imprint of a seal, most likely from a ring used some two thousand years ago," Alex answered.

Ronita cast a look of surprise at Matt before letting her mouth divulge what her mind had conceived.

"You can tell that just from looking at this photo?" she said suspiciously.

"I told you she was good," Matt whispered to Ronita before turning his attention back to Alex.

"What else?"

"Back then it was common for the prefects and rulers to use imprints crafted from different metals like copper, clay, silver and gold to seal papyrus documents that carried significant importance. The metal that was used was determined by the rank of the particular official—prefects used clay or copper, high priests used silver, and gold was reserved only for the kings, often including precious stones or gems in the design. Each seal was specially designed and crafted for that particular official or ruler's exclusive use, like a logo. They'd then seal an important document by pressing the ring onto wax or soft clay, like on the scroll in this picture. Often the seals also contained messages or phrases associated with that particular delegate, but it's impossible to make out if that was the case here from this photograph," Alex said.

"That's what I was afraid you'd say. Local authorities wouldn't let us near the body to have a closer look at the imprint," Matt said.

Ronita flipped through the folder they'd got from Ravid.

"There's nothing in here that suggests they might have found a ring in the room or anywhere in our vic's belongings."

"What would this ring be worth?" Matt asked Alex.

"Not enough to kill someone over, that's for sure, depending on who the ring belonged to, I'd say you're most likely looking at it being nothing more than a museum piece or a nice-to-have for a private jewelry collector," she answered.

"So you're saying this marking on our vic's body was made by a two-thousand-year-old ring. How's that even possible?" Ronita queried.

"I think I can help with that," Sam said. "It was most likely done at the time of the incident. When blood is forced out into the surrounding tissues after vascular disruption, in this case as a result of trauma or impact to the arm, it typically results in bruising. Often this bruising only shows up on the surface of the skin days after time of death. Judging from the yellowish color of this imprint, I'd estimate this photo was taken roughly three to five days after he died."

"So you're saying his arm made contact with the ring at the time of his death?" Matt asked.

"Correct. He could have either fallen against it or his attacker wore it, but my money's on the former. The subcutaneous bruising indicates gravitational force," Sam continued.

"So he fell on it," Matt clarified.

"Most likely, yes. His weight would have been significant enough to inflict the imprint if the object was trapped between his body and a hard surface like the floor. But there's more," Sam mocked, in the tone they use on the infomercials. "See these bruises over here? Those are fingerprints and they were left at the same time. So, my guess is, whoever was with him lifted his arm after he fell on top of the ring; quite possibly to remove the ring from under his weight."

Matt moved over to his place by the window, taking a moment to digest the new information before he addressed Red.

"Any sign of the Luke kid?"

"Negative. Ravid's men are out searching along the road leading away from the Old City but no news yet."

"Stay on it. My guess is this Luke boy took the ring and our killers are now after him. Ronita, stay here with Red and see if you can track down more images of the seal and send me the coordinates of the cave where they found the scroll. See if you can find out if the two students might have visited the cave on one of their tours." Matt grabbed his denim jacket and checked the clip on his gun before securing it back in its holster under his arm.

"Where are you going?" Ronita asked Matt as he beckoned for Alex and Sam to follow him.

"We're going to do Ravid's job for him. We need to find that kid before they kill him too," Matt answered as the trio left the hotel headquarters.

CHAPTER 5

When Matt parked his hired car in the small lot outside the Dung Gate on the southeast corner of the Old City, Alex readied her handgun and stuck it back into its usual place in the small of her back. Sam followed suit.

"So this is where Luke was last spotted on this camera over here, right?" Sam checked with Matt where he now stood below the surveillance camera.

"Yes. It's the only one at this entrance and shows him running down the road in this direction." Matt pointed at the road leading away from the Old City.

"How fast could he have run with cars and buses passing by? He couldn't have made it that far on foot," Alex said before the three of them set off down the road.

When they had already walked a solid five minutes, Sam shared his thoughts.

"I don't see any traces of blood anywhere."

"I'm going to take that as positive and assume the guy is still alive then," replied Matt.

"There are footprints over here," Alex interrupted from where she had stopped in front of a spot where the shoulder of the tarmac road gave way to sand, "and judging from the spacing between each step I'd say he was definitely still running. Perhaps a car forced him off the road," Alex ventured while she traced the footprints along the low wall with the fence before she stopped where the gaping hole in the fence stared back at her.

"Here!" she said with excitement as she pulled a piece of pale blue cotton from an exposed wire in the fence.

"That matches the shirt he was wearing in the surveillance footage," Matt stated.

"I say we see where it leads. I don't believe in coincidences," Sam announced.

"You're right. It makes perfect sense that he might have tried to escape through a hole in a fence if he couldn't outrun them," Alex agreed with Sam's assumption.

"Ladies first," Matt joked, bending at the waist while stretching out his arm for Alex to pass through the fence first; his gesture confirming their decision.

"And there you go making me look bad again. Thanks a lot, buddy," Sam joked.

"Always treat a Sheila like a lady, Sam. No matter how many guns she packs," Matt replied wryly.

"You talk as if you have experience. I'm assuming your gentlemanly charms stand you in good stead when you get back to your wife," Alex said, looking back at Matt when he purposefully avoided the question and instead stopped to investigate a fictitious clue in the dirt by his feet.

Noticing Alex's question had clearly made Matt uncomfortable, Sam cleared his throat and drew their attention to where skid marks lay in the sand in front of him.

"It seems the lad might have slipped and slid down the hill. Looks like he might have landed somewhere down there by that big boulder."

Welcoming the new lead, Matt didn't waste any time and set off toward the large rock halfway down the mound.

"What's with him," Alex whispered to Sam.

"Not sure, but whatever it is, it was triggered by you mentioning his wife. It's obviously a sensitive topic so let's cut him some slack, shall we? Besides, it's not really any of our business," Sam whispered back before Alex and he set off after Matt to where he was already hunched next to the rock.

"What do you make of this?" Matt asked pointing to a single drop of blood in the sand.

"Well, it's blood all right, but hardly anything to indicate that he was badly injured," Sam answered.

"I'm guessing this thorn had something to do with it," Alex said lifting up the sharp-pointed piece of wood where more blood had dried on one end.

"Is it poisonous?" Matt asked.

"It looks to me like a thorn from the *Ziziphus spina-christi*, otherwise known as *Christ's thorn*," Alex said.

"Wait, you're saying it's the plant used to make the crown that was placed upon Jesus' head during His crucifixion?" Sam queried.

"One and only. It's a popular evergreen shrub in these parts and a local source of food and medicine. Look." Alex pointed out several trees scattered along the hill and down into the valley below.

"So Luke might have rolled down the hill and hit that bush over there before this boulder broke his fall," Matt observed as he stood staring down toward the valley.

"I reckon it saved his life. The next rock would have killed him instantly," Sam pointed to a much larger boulder that bore a protruding sharp edge that lay about twenty feet away.

"Well, there's nothing else around here, so I'm assuming he might have been knocked unconscious and woke up here the next day," Alex suggested.

"Assuming you're correct, let's head back up to the road and carry on. There's bound to be more footprints," Matt said.

F urther along the road, with only the odd print left in the sand at one spot, the trio paused and Matt spoke.

"There's nothing here. He couldn't have gone this far. Where would a guy his age hide?"

"Perhaps they got to him, or he managed to hitch a ride into the village down there," Sam guessed.

"I think I know where he went," Alex announced, leaving a waft of excitement behind as she hastily moved forward and pointed in the direction of the ruins.

"It's not unlikely. It looks deserted enough for him to hide in. It's worth a try," Matt said, but Alex was already speeding down the embankment towards the ruins.

When her two male colleagues finally caught up with her they found her staring at the ancient structure with awe.

"What exactly are we looking at here?" Matt asked, still trying to catch his breath while rolling up his sleeves.

"You're looking at an ancient temple roughly fifteen hundred years old," Alex said grinning from ear to ear. "It's remarkable. I read about an excavation like this several years ago. Construction workers accidentally discovered it while working on a new residential neighborhood."

"You mean like this one," Sam asked, pointing at a nearby construction site.

"Exactly," Alex answered.

"What's with all the swimming pools?" Matt asked.

"You really don't know biblical history do you?" Alex said with surprise. "They're not swimming pools. They were most likely used as baptismal baths or for cleansing prior to entering the temple. There's not a lot of concrete evidence to support it but several other temples, like, for example, Solomon's Temple have the same trademarks. We know from past written records that the Jewish faith required Jews to cleanse themselves before entering the temples to worship."

"I agree that's fascinating, Sheila, but we need to crack on if we're to find Luke. What made you say he came here?"

"Your face for one," Alex said mysteriously.

"My face? What's my chiseled jaw got to do with anything?" Matt replied with a sheepish grin.

"Actually, it's the rivers of sweat and your tomato-like coloring that tipped me off," Alex teased in reply.

Sam exploded with laughter. "I don't think she's referring to your rugged looks, mate."

"I don't get it then," Matt commented, unable to figure it out.

"You're hot, and I don't mean it in the attractive sense of the word. This guy was on the run for what seems to have been at least two days. He would have been tired, hungry, hot and thirsty. We trailed his steps to where he had tumbled down the hill and landed against the boulder where, since it was nighttime and provided the perfect hiding place, I assume he would have spent the night. Since his position would have left him completely exposed during the day, it's clear he took his chances and went back up. For the most part, human behaviors are similar which suggests, since you stopped to rest, it's possible he did too. With the sun's positioning and from where he stood in the road, he would have seen this structure the same way we caught sight of it. Look around you. You have desert-like surroundings and in the midst of it, these ruins with a visibly green patch of oasis-like grass showing off a lush green fig tree."

"Water and food. He realized he'd find water and food here," Matt said.

"Precisely, and it wasn't long ago either. I found a pile of fresh fig skins under the tree and your 'swimming pool's' damp base is from the slow stream of water that's flowing from the pipe above it." Alex conveyed her findings.

Matt jumped down into the recessed basin and popped his head under the cool, barely visible, stream of water, pausing to take a few sips here and there.

"Just as smart as I remember. You're right. That's what any sane person on the run would do," Matt agreed when he eventually stepped away from the water.

"Question is though, where's the lad now?" Sam asked.

"They found him before we did," Matt answered in a somber tone where he now stood under the large fig tree examining the fresh footprints.

"I see at least three sets of footprints," Sam remarked.

"And signs of a struggle. The guy never stood a chance," Matt said.

"I wouldn't be so sure. Looks like he might have gotten away. Look here," Alex called them over and pointed at the single trail of shoe prints similar to the ones she had found at the shoulder of the road. Her eyes followed the tracks down to where it seemed to be heading towards the nearby construction site where a small group of men were at work alongside a small digger.

"Let's go check it out," Sam responded.

"We need to be careful. Men like these can easily be convinced to turn a blind eye," Matt cautioned.

"In that case we should use it to our advantage and offer them a little bonus of our own," Alex suggested.

"We can try, but tread carefully and stay alert," Matt warned again, and unclipped his gun's holster in preparation for a quick draw.

When they reached the bottom of the hill, a few of the men quickly turned and disappeared behind a nearby building site container as if they sensed trouble. Moments later a medium-built Israeli man flanked by two more men stepped out from behind the container.

"You're trespassing," the man announced.

"We're not looking for trouble. We just want to talk," Matt answered.

The man didn't respond, so a somewhat reluctant Matt tried again.

"We're looking for one of our friends, a young Australian man. He got separated from our group two nights ago and we think he might have lost his way and ended up down here. We were hoping you might have seen him."

The man had a quiet presence about him but the danger that lurked in his black eyes was hard to miss. He spat on the ground in front of him before he spoke.

"We haven't seen anyone."

"He's lying through his teeth," Alex whispered through a clenched jaw.

"Take it easy, Alex. He already has us surrounded," Sam whispered using his eyes to draw Matt and Alex's attention to the two dozen armed workers that had quietly sneaked into position around them.

"Okay, that's alright then. I'm sure he must have made it back to the hotel by now. Thank you for your time," Matt said as he slowly turned to leave.

"We'll make it worth your while." Alex's voice sliced through the air sending shockwaves through Matt's body.

"Have you lost your mind, Alex? We need to go!" Matt confronted her but she ignored him and continued.

"Everyone has a price, mister. What's yours?" she said.

"Alex, stop. This man will shoot us dead on the spot. Sam, speak to your foolish wife before she gets us killed," Matt's tense voice begged.

"She knows what she's doing, mate."

The Israeli man's silent gaze sent chills down Matt's spine while his eyes frantically searched for a way out from the surrounding army's aim.

"I know he's here. I'm prepared to offer you a trade," Alex said.

"I hope you know what you're doing, Sheila. And I don't even want to ask what you intend trading," Matt said, even more nervous than before. But his tension soon dissipated with the Israeli's response.

"I'm listening."

"I want to see him first," Alex challenged.

Matt's rigid body went just about limp under the weight of Alex's demand. He cast a watchful eye in Sam's direction whose face, instead of fear, displayed a sneaky smile in support of his wife's negotiations.

"You've both lost your minds," he muttered under his breath, as he readied himself to go for his gun.

"Wait for it," Sam whispered, and mere moments later the Israeli man muttered something to one of his men.

When shortly after, a badly beaten and tethered Luke was shoved to his knees in front of them, Matt's face said it all.

CHAPTER 6

"Your turn," the Israeli man replied.

"Oh great, now what?" Matt mumbled under his breath.

"Tell your men to stand down," Alex bargained.

"Don't waste my time, woman. Show me what you have to offer," the man ignored her plea.

As if it wasn't possible for Matt's body to tense up even more it did as he stood dead still under the Israeli man's dark gaze. He glanced at Sam who looked far too relaxed for his liking.

"Alex, what are you doing? You're not going to be able to bluff our way out of this one," Matt whispered sideways as he watched her hand disappear into her backpack.

Alex ignored him while her hand searched the inside of her bag.

"I'm taking it out now," she announced calmly, to ward off any hostile reaction from his henchman.

Amidst the dead silent pause that lay thick in the air across the small construction site, Matt exhaled a heavy sigh of relief when his eyes settled on the foot-long ancient pottery horse figurine in Alex's outstretched hand.

From roughly thirty feet away, where the Israeli man stood with Luke still kneeling in front of him, the man's faint gasp told Alex her plan had worked.

"Told you," Sam whispered to Matt.

The Israeli's sudden command to one of his men to have him take the statue from Alex rippled through the silent space between them.

"Uh-uh, not so fast." Alex stopped him, forcing Matt's back to stiffen again.

"Tell your men to lower their guns, and untie our friend. He can't walk with his hands and feet shackled. Once he reaches us I'll toss the statue to you and we'll forget this ever happened."

Alex held the man's gaze. Behind her brave exterior her heart pounded hard against her chest. She knew full well her behavior was risky. Now that he'd seen the ancient relic, nothing prevented him from having his men kill them all on the spot and taking it either way. They were entirely surrounded and clearly outnumbered. Next to her, even Sam had now tensed up under the pressure of the situation. She held her position and prepared herself for the worst. But the man didn't budge. He needed more motivation, she thought.

"Let our friend go and I'll tell you where to find more of these. His life isn't worth anything to you. Trading one of these statues on the black market on the other hand is," she said, making sure her voice didn't betray the fear that suddenly lay heavy in the pit of her stomach.

A few seconds passed before the man finally instructed one of his men to free Luke. Alex, Sam and Matt watched as they helped Luke to his feet and shoved him toward them. With one of the men closely following behind Luke they waited as the space between them slowly decreased. Just a few more feet and Luke would be within their reach. Her heartbeat pulsed against her temples but she forced her eyes to remain locked with the Israeli man's. As soon as Sam leaned across and pulled Luke in behind his body, Alex tossed the statue to the handler.

"You got what you want, now where's the rest?" The man's voice carried his impatience through the quiet building site.

"Up there," Alex pushed her chin out towards the temple ruins they had just come from.

She nervously watched the man inspect the ancient pottery relic in his hands. It was now or never, she thought, and, for the first time, she slowly broke her gaze and turned to see where Sam and Matt held Luke up between them.

"We need to move now," she whispered an urgent instruction to them.

All the while, keenly conscious of the Israeli man and his henchmen around them, they walked away, picking up their pace the farther they got.

When they reached the nearby dirt road that led to the small village close by, and while Alex frantically searched for a getaway vehicle, Sam announced what he had been suspecting all along.

"It's a fake isn't it?"

"Yup," Alex confirmed.

"It's a fake? What were you thinking?" Matt panicked.

"Just keep moving, Matt. He hasn't caught onto it yet," Alex said calmly while rushing toward a car outside a nearby house.

"And now we're going to steal someone's car as well," Matt muttered. "You're going to get us killed, Alex, and may I remind you that I'm a government agent," he continued, still somewhat frantic about the possible repercussions of their bluff.

Alex ignored Matt's panicked rant as she yanked the dusty white car's door open and tucked her hands in underneath the steering wheel. Seconds later she had pulled the wires from the console and bypassed the ignition system.

"Get in!" she yelled.

In the rearview mirror she watched the Israeli construction team move up the hill toward the temple ruins. So far so good, her bluff had paid off. But it wouldn't take them long to realize she had fooled them.

"You know, they're going to find out you tricked them and they'll come for us," Matt said, when they managed to successfully get back to where he had parked his rental car at the Dung Gate.

"Relax, mate. He's not an archaeologist. Trust me. It will take him days before he realizes it's fake," Sam said as he settled next to Luke in the backseat of Matt's car.

But his words had barely left his lips when a bullet clanked loudly against the boot of Matt's car.

"You were saying," Matt yelled out, pushing his car over the sidewalk and through a small space between two moving tourist coaches.

The street surrounding the Old City was congested forcing them to stop for oncoming traffic. Aware of their assailants' approaching silver pickup truck behind them, his thumb hit the hands-free dial button on his steering wheel. Red's upbeat voice sounded on the other end of the phone line.

"Get us out of here, Red," Matt instructed.

"On it, boss," the computer tech replied.

A mere two seconds later he was back on the phone.

"Take the next turn left and keep it steady at twenty miles per hour for seven seconds then speed up to fifty. You'll clear both traffic lights. Then head east around the city back to HQ. I've cleared the way."

"You've got to keep them off our tail, Red," Matt continued.

"Already taken care of, boss. I've created a little entertainment to keep our friends occupied."

Matt didn't ask what. He trusted his team and followed Red's instructions to the tee, and it wasn't long before the distance between them and the silver pickup had increased. Red's so-called 'entertainment' involved a short circuit with several traffic lights that caused a massive traffic jam and several fender benders. By the time Matt's car had reached the eastbound route back to the hotel headquarters, they had successfully escaped.

"We've lost them, Matt," Sam informed him.

But Matt's usual happy-go-lucky manner gave way to a stern tone. "You almost had us killed with that idiotic move of yours, Alex," he said.

"But it didn't," Alex replied.

"Thanks to Red, yes! You put my entire team in danger. This isn't some Lone Ranger mission, Alex."

Alex knew Matt meant business when he chose to use her real name instead of calling her Sheila.

"There's no way we could have known he'd figure it out so quickly, Matt. It worked and we got Luke out safely," Sam argued back.

"These guys know when they see a forged relic, Sam. They're seasoned smugglers."

"Well we lost them, we're in the clear," Sam defended again.

"And how long do you think that will last, huh? My entire team's lives are now in jeopardy."

"We'll watch our backs and make sure they don't track us to the hotel. Once we get Luke out of here and safely back home they'll eventually give up trying to find us," Sam said.

"Let's hope you're right," Matt added.

"Sorry, Matt. It was a risk, I know, but I couldn't just leave Luke there. I knew they had him. Once they handed him to Nathan's killers they would've killed him too and you know it. It was only a matter of time. We saved his life," Alex spoke with a gentle tone.

"I get it, Sheila. Apology accepted. Just don't do something stupid like that again, okay? I don't have much of a life to lose but Red and Ronita are young and it's my responsibility to see they stay safe. How's he doing?" Matt changed the subject when he caught a glimpse of where Luke lay in a semi-conscious state in his back seat.

"He's dehydrated and was beaten to a pulp but he'll survive. A day or two in the hospital and he'll be ready to head home," Sam answered.

"Hospital! No way that can happen now. You'll have to work your magic at the hotel. He's as good as dead if word gets out of his whereabouts," said Matt.

"I see your point. It will take longer without an I.V. but I can do it the old-fashioned way. As long as he stays conscious," Sam replied.

Matt glanced at Alex next to him.

"So, are you going to tell me or not?" he asked her.

"Tell you what?" she said, puzzled.

"What's the deal with the fake figurine and why were you carrying it around with you?"

"Nothing. It was simply something I had picked up at the airport curio shop. It reminded me of a relic my father had discovered during an excavation in Greece when I was a child. This was a near exact replica of an ancient ritual figurine that was recently discovered at Tel Motza. I knew he'd recognize it since it was all over the news. They had discovered quite a few but some of them went missing a few months ago. It was the perfect bait and all I could think of in that moment."

"Well, you certainly had me fooled, Sheila. Remind me not to ever play poker with you," Matt laughed as he parked his pickup in the hotel parking lot.

"Take him up. I'll get rid of the car," Matt instructed.

CHAPTER 7

"How's he doing?" Matt asked when he entered their hotel headquarters.

"He'll be okay. It's best to let him rest for a few hours," Sam reported, closing the bedroom door behind him.

"Has he said anything yet?"

Sam shook his head. "He's quite shaken up. They got to him good and proper."

"Do you think they were the ones behind Nathan's murder?" Alex asked.

"I doubt it. They're too exposed out there. Not to mention that they gave him up in a heartbeat. If he were of any real value to them they would have held onto him. I think they accidentally found Luke at the ruins and thought they'd try their luck at ransoming him. But since that would've involved a substantial amount of patience and risk, the prospect of a bigger payoff with Alex's fake artifact proved the easier option."

"Boss, we have visitors," Red reported from behind his wall of computers where he had hacked into the hotel's surveillance cameras.

Matt leaned in over Red's shoulder.

"It's Ravid." Matt nervously scratched the back of his head before allowing his eyes to scan the room.

"Not a word about Luke. Sam, keep an eye on the boy and make sure he stays quiet should he wake up," he instructed, moments before Ravid knocked on the door.

Pausing briefly after Sam disappeared into the bedroom, Matt answered the door.

"To what do we owe the pleasure, Ravid?" Matt asked as the Israeli detective let himself in.

"Taylor," he greeted, then continued, "just thought I'd pop by and see if you've managed to find anything."

"I was hoping you'd have the autopsy report for me, actually. These pictures are no good," Matt replied, evading the detective's question.

"Not yet but we should have it by the end of the week."

Ravid's eyes scanned the room and settled on where Alex had busied herself next to Ronita on her laptop.

"This is Alex. She's an industry colleague helping me with this case," Matt introduced.

"Colleague, huh. And what industry would that be exactly?"

"Artifact and antiquity recovery, over in the UK. I flew her in to help find whatever it was that caused the marking on our vic's arm."

"Isn't that why you're here?" Ravid asked suspiciously.

"We go hand in hand really. She recovers the artifact and I take down the traffickers, assuming we have any of course. Just like you're supposed to find the murderers, come to think of it. See, teamwork."

Ravid's angry eyes let Matt know that his sarcasm had hit a chord. They were clearly a thorn in his flesh and if Matt didn't know any better, he'd have said Ravid was hiding something. Any normal officer of the law would have jumped at the opportunity to have a specialized team help him solve a high-profile murder case. But not Ravid.

"Speaking of which, any leads yet?" Matt pushed again.

"Not yet. Forensics is still busy with the bullet casings found in the room and on the stairwell."

"And the boy, have you found him?" Matt cast his bait.

"Not yet, but I have witnesses who said they saw him in a village just outside the Old City. It won't take me long to find him."

"In that case, how about you let us get on with our jobs then."

Ravid's eyes narrowed before he turned as if to walk to the door and then stopped.

"There was quite the commotion in town earlier. Gunshots, traffic jams and a couple of really angry construction workers saying some foreigners scammed them. You don't happen to know anything about that, do you?" Ravid's dark eyes were fixed on Matt's face as he waited for him to answer.

"Gunshots, really? Seems your city is running wild, Ravid," Matt's clever answer came back.

Neither of the two men spoke while they held their gaze. Unspoken messages of suspicion, distrust and dislike exchanged between them in a silent duel before Ravid turned and left the room.

Matt moved across the room to Red's computer monitors and watched Ravid and his men until they exited the hotel.

"Think he knows something?" Ronita asked.

"Knows, no. Suspects, yes," Matt answered from where he now stood at the window staring down at them in the street below.

But Matt carried his own suspicions. "Red, see what you can find out about our detective friend, in particular his past cases. See if there's anything involving stolen artifacts and so on, and be discreet. I don't want anything leading back to us."

"You think he's dirty?" Alex commented.

"Not sure, but I do know enough about the human psyche to know that his frustration over our involvement in this case stems from something far more complicated than a foreign team of investigators on his turf."

"I agree with you, Matt. His visit was a fishing expedition and not just a casual pop-in. I doubt he knows we have Luke though. He would have searched the place," Alex said.

"Speaking of, our lad's awake." Sam stuck his head out of the bedroom.

When Alex and Matt joined Sam, next to where a badly bruised Luke now sat up in the bed, Matt spoke first.

"Hey, Luke, I'm Matt. How are you feeling, mate?"

A faint smile came across the injured young man's face.

"You're Australian," he observed.

"A pure-bred, NSW boy, yes."

"New South Wales," Sam whispered to Alex when Matt's abbreviation puzzled her.

"You're from Canberra I understand," Matt stated, to which Luke nodded.

"I'm from Port Macquarie. Not far from you... lived there all my life." Matt paused before he continued in a more somber tone.

"I'm sorry about Nathan. I understand you've been friends for a very long time."

Luke nodded.

"He didn't deserve to die like that. What happened?" Matt continued.

Luke's eyes moved from Matt to Sam, and then Alex, before he looked back at Sam.

"It's okay, Luke. You can trust us. We want to find whoever did this to the two of you," Sam reassured.

Luke's hand slowly reached into the pocket of his pants before he steadily pulled an object out and held his closed fist against his chest. The sad expression on his beaten-up face declared the guilt and regret that lay behind the object in his hand.

"It's all my fault," he said with a quiver in his voice.

"No it's not. You didn't pull the trigger, Luke," Sam said.

"I might as well have. He told me not to take it."

"What?" Matt probed.

"Who told you not to take what, Luke?" Matt pushed harder when Luke fell silent.

"Nathan. He told me not to take this." Luke opened his fist and allowed the team's eyes to run over the silver ring in the palm of his shaky hand.

"May I?" Alex asked, and gently took the ring from him.

"This is why they killed Nathan and are now after you?" Matt confirmed.

Luke nodded.

"That's it?" Matt asked, sounding slightly insensitive.

"I don't understand. Apart from the fact that we've found what caused the imprint on Nathan's arm, I fail to see why this ring is valuable enough to kill two students over." Matt declared his thoughts out loud sounding frustrated and disappointed.

"Where did you find it?" Alex asked Luke.

"In the forest. The Peace Forest," he repeated when Alex frowned.

"What do you mean you found it? Just lying on the ground?" Alex asked.

"Not exactly. We were part of a tour group going through the forest, a walking tour. I was bored so I persuaded Nathan to deviate from the group, just for a bit and we'd catch up with them a bit later." Luke fell silent as his mind recalled the memory.

"Go on," Alex nudged.

"We went off the trail and through the trees. I heard it was a shortcut to where the Second Temple period graves are. It wasn't part of the tour—apparently old people don't like hanging out in graveyards. Nathan didn't want to either." Luke paused again.

"And that's where you found the ring, in the graveyard," Matt prompted impatiently which yielded a cautionary glance from Alex.

"Yes, sort of. Nathan told me that the graves were haunted and that we'd only be safe if we were inside a circle. He said he read it somewhere."

"So you carved out a circle in the soil and then found the ring," Alex asked.

Luke nodded. "I should have never taken it. Nathan told me not to take it. Now he's dead and it's all my fault."

Matt paced the room, ignoring the young man's guilty confession. "Okay, so he found a ring. People find all kinds of ancient pieces of pottery and stuff all over Israel and Syria all the time. Why kill over it? Looks like a normal piece of old jewelry to me."

"I'd have to clean it up a bit more to be sure but it doesn't strike me as normal," Alex said.

"Oh? Why not?" Matt asked.

"Well, to start, it's definitely made of silver. Silver was a precious metal reserved only for high-ranking officials back then. Whoever this ring belonged to must have had power."

Matt folded his arms across his chest and stared at Luke.

"Would you be able to find the place again?"

Luke nodded, even though he loathed the idea of going back there.

"We'll have to do it at night. We can't risk being followed or seen during broad daylight. The place is crawling with tourists and I'm pretty certain Ravid has us under eyes." He paused next to Luke again. "Think you're up to doing it tonight?"

"You want to go crawling around a haunted graveyard in the middle of a forest at night?" Alex said, somewhat alarmed.

"Carpe diem, Sheila, carpe diem. Besides, you don't really believe in all that stuff do you? Look at it this way. At least we don't have to go crawling around in a cave."

CHAPTER 8

Matt's question still rippled through her mind as Alex stepped onto the barely distinguishable forest path and fell in line behind Luke. She didn't believe in ghosts but it was well past midnight and the forest was eerily dark and deathly quiet. The cool spring breeze rustled lightly through the thick foliage above their heads.

They had climbed over the large iron gate at the entrance to the Peace Forest while Red jammed the signals of the only two security cameras above the gate. He had cautioned them against three night watchmen who patrolled the larger public areas with their dogs.

"Keep your eyes open for the security guards. It's the last thing we need right now. The less I see of Ravid the better," Matt said.

The unofficial brown leafy trail crunched beneath their feet as they steadily walked the slight slope down toward where the graveyard was located about a quarter of a mile ahead. She could understand why Luke and Nathan had deviated from the tour group. During the day it would certainly hold a tranquil allure in the middle of a city that was barren for the most part. At night, not so much. To the side, above her head, Alex noticed a long-eared owl curiously staring back at them. Unimpressed with the untimely human interruption to his nocturnal hunt, he suddenly flew off and snatched a small unsuspecting rodent from between the dry foliage on the ground before disappearing with it into the branches of a large pine tree.

As if their night investigation would have been incomplete without it, a faint cloud of white haze had gathered at the foot of the slope. Peeking out from behind it, the ancient stone graveyard slowly came into vision as they drew nearer.

"There it is. That's the graveyard," Luke announced, his voice drenched in melancholy.

"It wasn't your fault, lad." Sam spoke with a gentle tone beside him.

But Luke's heart remained heavy. For in that moment, he knew. Of all the idiotic things he'd done in his life, this one would torment him forever, and his best friend had paid the ultimate price for his childish stupidity.

"Show us where you found it, Luke, so we can catch whoever did this to him," Matt nudged, making every attempt to show empathy towards the student. Over the years his career at ASIO has taught him to suppress his emotions and not allow them to cloud his judgment, but he couldn't deny that part of him was angry with Luke for getting his friend killed.

"There, on the other side of that large tree." Luke pointed with his finger and proceeded to follow Matt and Alex down towards it. Luke welcomed Sam's calm reassuring presence behind him. But the feeling was short lived when Matt's forearm suddenly went into a ninety-degree upward fist and Alex and Sam simultaneously wedged Luke in a protective cocoon between them.

"Get down," Alex whispered, and reached for her gun before she moved into position behind Matt.

Sam pulled Luke down next to him behind the nearby brush and drew his gun also. Fixed to their spot between the trees they listened. Male voices drifted in the mist towards them. From where Alex and Matt now hid behind two tall pine trees, they locked eyes and silently communicated their observations. Three, maybe four. Not English. Maybe Hebrew, they couldn't tell. Alex placed her night-vision monocular in front of one eye and slowly moved the scope across their sightline. After a brief pause she confirmed four men standing next to one of the graves. Matt signaled for Sam to stay with Luke while he and Alex carefully moved forward. Using the thick tree trunks and shadowy corners of the forest, Alex and Matt closed in on where they now saw two of the men digging with shovels into the soft soil. Across the graveyard several shallow holes lay scattered; evidence they'd already been there for a while and were hunting for something specific. The sudden unexpected bark of a dog cast in their direction declared two certainties: the night watchmen were in on it and they'd been made.

Alex and Matt fell back behind two trees. Alex pinned her shoulders against the rough trunk, pushed her body deeper into the tree's shadow, and glanced carefully at where Matt had done the same. From behind the trees the men stopped digging while their eyes urgently searched the dark corners of the graveyard. The canine's neck pulled hard against his collar when his body veered against his handler's weight. He sent off three more barks in their direction. Alex cast a concerned glance to where Sam still sat hidden behind the brush with Luke by his side. The alarmed look in her husband's eyes confirmed that he knew they were in a vulnerable position. Alex drew her attention back to where the watchman allowed his dog to lead his master to their hiding place. Using her hands, Alex suggested to Matt that they should split up into opposite directions to lead the dog and handler away from Sam and Luke. Silent communication from Matt in response confirmed her diversion strategy was the best recourse and a rapid finger countdown set their game plan in motion.

The sudden muffled crackling from the dry leaves beneath their feet had the dog yank his handler forward in a panicked fit. With his dog's undeniable warning of intruders the guard relayed the message back to the group behind him. In unison, the four men dropped their shovels and simultaneously reached for their guns. Now armed and spaced out between the trees, they deployed into the forest in search of the threat. As planned, Alex and Matt bolted in opposite directions and away from Sam and Luke, which left the dog who had been sniffing the ground, dazed and confused. His body bounced back and forth between two opposing directions forcing his handler to unclip his collar from the leash. The dog made his choice and with his handler in close proximity behind him, darted off in the direction Matt had run.

On the other end, halfway up the gentle incline, Sam and Luke watched in angst as the four armed men advanced closer to where they were still trapped and unable to move out from behind the brush. Sam's eyes trailed Alex as she bolted through the trees to where she eventually disappeared in the shadows between rows of tall trees. From her determined movement he could tell she was executing an improvised phase of their original strategy that had somewhat backfired. Luke's quivering body and panicked eyes indicated the level of fear that ripped through his body when his sharp mind realized they were sitting ducks. The thought of getting caught and beaten again set about a series of shallow, anxious gasps that left his lungs begging for air.

"Breathe... relax," Sam mouthed, while he forced the young man to lock eyes with him. "We're going to be fine," he whispered.

In that moment, a dull thud preceded by a short series of similar sounding noises came from where the men had been digging in the graveyard moments before. The sudden intrusion on their hunting ground got precisely the reaction Alex had hoped for and within seconds two of the men charged back down the slope to the graveyard. With guns in hand they commenced their search between the five-foot-tall ancient stone columns that outlined the area. Seizing the opportunity, Sam yanked Luke to his feet, urging him to make a run toward a slightly more obscure hiding place behind a high stone wall that had broken away from the original ancient building some feet away. It worked, and they soon reached the safety of the ruin.

In the distance the dog's shrill yelps echoed through the night air informing Sam and Luke that Matt might have found a way to get the canine off his tail.

"See, we've got your back, mate," Sam announced proudly before he moved to where a narrow crack in the wall gave him the perfect view of the graveyard close by. The moon's reflection on the zipper on Alex's black leather jacket caught his eye and Sam watched as mere seconds later both men lay unconscious at her feet.

"That's my girl," he mumbled with a smile.

Sudden movement in the trees behind him instantly transformed his pride into fear and he spun around to see Matt appearing from the shadows.

"I almost shot you, mate!" Sam whisper-shouted.

"I'm glad you didn't. Is Alex okay?"

Sam nodded. "She got two of them but I haven't caught sight of the other two or the guard."

"Oh, they won't be coming for us anytime soon. I had a little help from a family of nocturnal friends. They'll be picking quills from their bodies until the sun comes up. Let's go find out what these guys have been up to, shall we?" Matt summoned.

They found Alex knelt next to her two unconscious victims between two large headstones. She had searched their bodies for anything that might give away their identities.

"Anything?" Sam asked.

"No, they're clean."

"No worries, Sheila. I'll have Red run facial mapping," Matt said as he captured the men's faces on his mobile phone and sent it off to his techie.

"Whatever they're after had them digging up holes all over the place, and I'm assuming this is the so-called safety circle you mentioned, Luke?" Sam queried where he stood over a perfectly round shallow hole next to one of the graves.

Luke nodded.

"Something doesn't add up though," Alex said before she continued. "How did they know about the circle or the ring for that matter? You said you and Nathan were alone. Did anyone else know about it, Luke?" Alex asked.

Luke dropped his head without answering.

"Luke, did you tell anyone?" She pushed again.

But before Luke could answer the question, a sudden rustling of leaves drew their attention to movement coming from the bushes behind them.

"We need to get him out of here," Matt whispered and drew his gun.

"I thought you said you dealt with the others," Sam said, somewhat annoyed.

"I did."

CHAPTER 9

Detective Ravid's face appeared from behind the bushes moments after his torchlight blinded Matt's eyes.

Taken by surprise there was little to no time to hide Luke from the Israeli detective's dark eyes.

"I should have known," he said to Matt. "What happened to teamwork, Taylor?"

Matt holstered his gun.

"What are you doing here, Ravid?" he diverted the question.

"What am *I* doing here? I should ask *you* that question. Have you forgotten you're in my jurisdiction, Taylor? And this is trespassing. It's the middle of the night and you're out here in a public park digging up dirt. I knew you were hiding something, or should I say someone? He's coming with me. Take him." Ravid instructed two of his men to cuff Luke.

"You're arresting him? On what grounds?" Alex challenged.

"Not that I owe any of you an explanation, but he was the last person to have seen the victim alive. I'm taking him in for questioning," Ravid answered.

"He's still an Australian citizen. He has rights," Matt reminded.

"And he will be given his rights. I suggest you follow your own advice and let me do my job of finding the killer while you focus on finding out what caused the marking on the victim's arm. I'm assuming that's what this is all about." Ravid turned to walk away. "And clean up this mess you made here before I arrest you for vandalism," he added as he and his men took Luke away and disappeared between the trees.

Matt paced the graveyard. Even in the pitch-black darkness of the night with only the moon's rays catching his face every so often it was evident Matt wasn't at all pleased by Ravid's unexpected visit.

"That was a close call. Am I happy we tied those two up behind that wall. Ravid could've arrested us too," Sam said in an attempt to cheer Matt up but instead, Matt continued pacing out his anger.

"Luke's probably better off with the police at this stage, Matt. At least he'll be safe while he's being detained." Alex tried to calm him down.

"I suppose you're right, except we're nowhere nearer to figuring this thing out. He clearly knew more than he let on."

"We have the ring and we know where he found it. We'll figure it out soon enough. Here," Alex handed Matt a shovel, "start digging."

T he night dragged on as Alex, Matt and Sam shoveled their way through the graveyard in search of anything that might explain the ring's origin.

"You know, we could go to hell for this," Matt said.

"For digging up soil?" Alex asked.

"It's a graveyard, Sheila. There's who knows how many dead bodies here. I would imagine it's best not to set the dead free."

"You watch way too many zombie movies, mate," Sam laughed.

"Says the doctor. Do you really need me to explain what happens when you disturb a soul? You of all people should know," Matt continued.

"Sounds to me like you're scared. Who would have known?" Alex teased.

"My grandmother taught me to respect the dead. Don't come crying to me when one jumps up from beyond the grave," Matt said.

"Well, mate, if I know one thing, then it's that that can't happen. Dead is dead and what's beneath the ground is nothing but bones. And as for what happened to their souls, well that depends on if they followed Christ or not."

Matt stopped digging and glanced at Sam.

"I didn't take you for the religious type, Sam. I must say, that's caught me by surprise."

"That's because I'm not. Being religious is one thing, but choosing salvation is entirely different. Make me one of your delicious bear stews and I'll tell you all about it," Sam bargained.

"That's a date. What about you, Sheila? Are you also a believer?"

Alex pushed her foot down onto the shovel and watched it sink away in the dirt.

"I'm warming up to the idea. It certainly intrigues me. Unlike Sam I wasn't raised in the church so wrapping my head around believing in some higher power isn't that simple. I guess I'd need proof that he existed."

"Spoken like a true scientist," Matt laughed. "And therein lies the conundrum. I'm told the very definition of faith is believing in that which is unseen."

"Well, look at you. Seems there's hope for you after all," Sam teased. "Sounds like our date's going to have to be stretched over a couple of days."

Alex stopped digging and rested her arm on the spade's handle. She shone her flashlight across the dozen holes that lay spread out throughout the ancient burial ground.

"I know. We're trying to find a needle in a haystack here," Matt commented as he too rested his tired arms and wiped his brow.

"Those two will wake up soon too, not to mention that their friends could come down that path at any moment." Sam added his thoughts.

Alex dropped her spade and started walking between the graves. They were right. They could be digging till the cows came home and not find anything that would shed light on where the ring came from. Pausing at a particular gravestone that seemed slightly separated from the rest, she allowed her eyes to take it in. Under her torch she recognized the writing to be Hebrew. She studied it carefully before she moved on to the next stone and then back to the first one. As she stared at the writing she noticed a similarity between the stones. Excitement flooded her insides and she dashed to the third, then the fourth and back to the first gravestone.

"What is it?" Sam said when he recognized his wife's reactions to indicate she was onto something.

"I think we could be one step closer to finding what we're looking for. Sam, take out that language app of yours and translate these lines here. Then check it against the rest of the stones," Alex said while moving to where she had dropped her shovel.

"Matt, start digging from that end and I'll start over here," she instructed.

"You want me to dig underneath the actual gravestone. Have you lost your mind? Did you not hear anything I said earlier? I don't intend on being eaten alive by dead people," he ranted.

"Are you hearing yourself, Matt? They're dead. They can't eat you. Now stop wasting time and start digging."

"Why, what makes you so sure you'll find whatever we're looking for on this spot?" Matt said.

Alex didn't answer. Instead she poked the ground several times with the metal part of her spade before she pushed the blade into the soil.

"Alex, you're a genius!" Sam exclaimed.

"Why, what are you talking about?" Matt said, feeling slightly left out.

"We're looking at graves from the Second Temple period, right?" Sam said.

"Is that supposed to mean anything?" Matt said, annoyed.

"The Second Temple period is when the Second Temple of Jerusalem existed and was a crucial part of Jewish history. It lasted between 516 BC and AD 70 coming to an end with the First Jewish-Roman War when the Romans destroyed Jerusalem and The Temple. All the major religious sects were formed during this period; Pharisees, Sadducees, Essenes and even early Christianity, and this particular grave is the only one inscribed as our deceased friend being a Sadducee. The rest are all Pharisees," Sam explained.

"And? What's that got to do with the ring?" Matt's confusion continued.

"How many Sadducee high priests do you know of that ruled in Judea during that time period?" Alex said.

"I think we've established my biblical knowledge leaves much to be desired. Stop playing games and tell me what's going on here." Matt's annoyance cut through the night air, interrupted only by the sudden dull thud that came from the ground beneath Alex's spade.

She paused, just briefly, before she pulled back on her shovel and gently pushed it into the soil again. Another thud echoed back. Alex found her heart skip several beats as she and Sam exchanged a look of excitement. Moments later they had fallen to their knees and ferociously started scooping handfuls of dirt away from the buried object.

"That had better be a box filled with treasure and not a centuries old corpse," Matt moaned.

"If it is, and if you want your share, you'd better start digging, mate," Sam teased.

It didn't take them long to dig up the buried box. On the edge of an ancient burial site, in the middle of the Peace Forest in Jerusalem, they quietly stared at their find. Measuring roughly fifteen inches high by about thirty inches long, they had lifted the limestone object out from beneath the dirt.

"Any guesses what we're looking at here?" Matt asked, feeling as paranoid as earlier.

Alex inspected the detailed etching, and moved her hand over the rich carvings of the circular patterns on the long side of the box. In direct contrast, on the narrow side, her fingers traced the deep etchings of eight Hebrew letters.

"On it," Sam announced, pre-empting the request to punch the symbols into his mobile phone's application. When the result came in a mere second later, Sam drew in a sudden shallow breath and without speaking, shoved the phone's screen in front of his wife's face.

"What? What is it?" Matt pushed impatiently as he watched Alex's face mirror the surprised look Sam now wore on his face.

"Pinch me," Alex whispered.

"I'll do more than pinch you both if you don't tell me what we're looking at here," Matt's voice jerked the couple back to reality.

Alex stared into Matt's curious eyes.

"This, my friend, is an ossuary containing the remains of Joseph, son of Caiaphas, otherwise known to us as Caiaphas."

CHAPTER 10

"Y ou're not bringing that box into our HQ. It's bad enough you're making me carry it around in my car," Matt said as they drove away from the forest.

"Why, scared it's going to jump out and eat your face off?" Alex chafed.

"Mock me all you want. I know what I know. Where I come from it's bad luck to dig up graves."

"Relax. I won't open the lid... yet," Alex poked again, which solicited a spout of laughter from her and Sam.

"Very funny, but seriously now. What are we supposed to do with a container full of some ancient priest's bones?" Matt asked.

"Do you even know what we have here, Matt?" Sam asked, in awe of Matt's ignorant comment.

"Not a clue, but I have a feeling you're about to tell me," Matt snickered.

"Ever heard of Pontius Pilate? He was the Roman prefect who consented to Jesus Christ's crucifixion. Caiaphas was his high priest, the very man responsible for having Jesus crucified," Alex explained.

"That makes no sense. Why would a priest have a holy man crucified?" Matt said confused.

"The very two reasons that exist in governments all over the world today: power and money. Being a high priest had very little to do with religion and everything to do with politics. Back then the high priest held the majority seat in the Sanhedrin, their supreme court so to speak. They were wealthy and incredibly involved in politics. Their wealth mostly came from charging taxes and exploiting the people, especially in the temples. They charged for everything, from entrance fees into the temple to having to pay to take a cleansing bath before they were even allowed to worship. So when a humble carpenter's son came riding into town on a donkey, claiming he was the son of God, going around prophesying, raising people from the dead, healing the sick and preaching messages of hope, people stopped going to the temples and followed him instead."

"So Caiaphas lost money," Matt concluded.

"Exactly, and having an empty temple during Passover, the busiest time of the year would be like Wall Street crashing," Sam continued.

"So he needed to get rid of him," Matt said.

"Yup, by using his influence, fabricating false testimonies and breaking the judicial trial laws. It was a cold, calculating move of political convenience. But he had nothing on Jesus to have him killed, except blasphemy, which in itself wasn't a crime worthy enough of crucifixion. Back in AD 33 very few people in Jerusalem considered Jesus holy. Jerusalem was the religious capital where only God Himself was considered holy. So when this seemingly ordinary man came into town claiming to be the Messiah, Caiaphas seized the opportunity and imposed his power on Pilate who, according to scripture, grudgingly agreed. What Caiaphas didn't realize, was that his evil actions actually fulfilled God's plan for Jesus' death, the very prophecy Jesus had been speaking of all along. Only after He was crucified and resurrected, performing many more miracles in the flesh all across Judea, did they realize He'd been telling the truth all along."

Matt went quiet behind the wheel as he contemplated the biblical account that Sam had given. "You're right, we're going to need more than one date."

"Circling us back to the ring. I have a strong suspicion that the ring Luke found must have belonged to Caiaphas himself. We've already determined the ring was an ancient insignia used to seal important documents, and since it was cast in silver, which was the metal reserved for royal officials only, it's fair to assume that it belonged to someone with substantial power close to the governor. If Caiaphas was as powerful as Sam says he was, it must have been his. Of course, there's only one way we can be certain; we'd have to somehow get the contents of this container analyzed, and as much as I'd like for us to take credit for this remarkable discovery, we can't. It would raise too many questions and unnecessary attention," Alex explained.

"What do you suggest we do?" Sam asked.

"The only thing we can do right now. We're going to make an anonymous delivery to the Israel Museum."

"Anything on our graveyard friends yet?" Matt asked his team when they walked back into their hotel headquarters two hours later.

"Nothing yet, boss. I'm still scanning the local databases and have just included social media," Red answered.

"But we did get a call from Ravid," Ronita informed him.

Matt groaned.

"He has some questions around a grave robbery that occurred in the Peace Forest last night. He said you'd know exactly what he's talking about. Apparently they found two of the thieves tied up behind a wall," Ronita continued, casting a suspicious eye at her boss.

"You didn't say anything about stealing from graves, boss," Red said sounding concerned.

"Unfortunately, it had to be done. But don't worry, I have it on good authority that zombies don't exist," Matt said as he poured himself a fresh cup of coffee.

"So what did you dig up then?" Ronita asked.

"The owner of the ring. At least I'm fairly certain he was. We found an ancient ossuary with a single Hebrew inscription on it. You'll need to keep an eye on any news coming from the Israel Museum over the next few days or so, please, Ronita. We were forced to make an anonymous donation to the museum vault," Alex divulged.

"So whose ring is it?" Red asked.

"Caiaphas," Alex said with confidence.

"The high priest who had Jesus killed," Ronita said, causing Matt to spit a mouthful of coffee across the floor.

"*You* know who he was?" Matt said in surprise, once he caught his breath.

"Of course, who doesn't?"

It took every bit of self-control for Alex and Sam not to laugh out loud but as hard as they tried they couldn't.

"Face it, mate, I clearly have my work cut out with you. But fear not, hope is a wonderful thing and that's something I have tons of," Sam joked.

"Found them!" Red came to Matt's rescue.

"Meet Hassan Bahar and Akram Najjar. Both Syrian nationals suspected of multiple counts of weapons trafficking. Neither has ever been convicted."

Red flashed two images across the large flat screen.

"Weapons smuggling, are you sure?" Alex queried.

"Affirmative, the system doesn't lie," Red confirmed.

Matt scanned over the information documents that replaced the two photos on the screen.

"That explains why the security guards were in on it," he said.

"You think they're using the graveyard to conceal weapons? It's brilliant if you think of it. I mean what sane person goes around digging up ancient burial grounds?" Alex said as she and Sam exchanged a mocking look.

Matt flashed a sarcastic smile. "Except I never saw any weapons of any kind anywhere."

"Maybe we interrupted them before they retrieved them," Sam ventured.

"If they were there to pick up weapons, wouldn't they know exactly where to dig? There were holes all over the place. I don't buy it. They were looking for something else and they had no idea where it was," Matt concluded.

"I think you're right, Matt. Luke also didn't recognize any of them, which tells me they weren't the ones who shot Nathan and then chased after him. It could just be a coincidence and totally unrelated to the ring." Sam filled his coffee mug for the second time.

"Except they are related," Red reported from behind his screens again.

"Explain," Matt invited.

"They're linked to four other men. All of whom are also Syrian. And get this, convicted of weapons trafficking and Middle-Eastern antiquity theft."

"So they were there on a treasure hunt," Ronita voiced what the rest of the team already knew.

"How do two students on holiday from Australia get themselves smack bang in the middle of an illegal art trade?" Sam asked.

"That's what we're here to find out, mate," Matt said from where he now stood with his hands on his hips staring out the hotel window again.

"I guess we know the answer to my question then," Alex said.

"Yup. It seems obvious now that they did tell someone else about the ring. They must have. The questions we need answering now are who and why?" Matt said before turning to face Ronita.

"Ronita, see if you can get anything more out of Ravid. Perhaps he has a lead or found witnesses we could follow up on. We also need to find out what else Luke isn't telling us. Push Ravid for a visit with him. Use our 'legal obligation to our citizens' card and if that doesn't work, threaten him with calling the minister. The last thing he'd want is his prime minister breathing down his neck."

"I'll go with her," Sam offered, "the lad trusts me."

"Good idea," Matt authorized.

"And I'm off to see one of my father's old colleagues. He used to work for the Israel Antiquities Authority but retired a few years ago. He keeps himself occupied with the odd off-the-record case and has a small lab set up at his house. I'd like to run some tests on the ring and see if it 'speaks' to me. There's got to be more to it than meets the naked eye," Alex said.

"Sounds good. Keep us posted. I'll see what Red and I can find out about our Syrian friends and we'll regroup here in three hours. Watch your backs," Matt cautioned.

CHAPTER 11

Alex paused when she stepped out of the hotel lobby into the somewhat quiet street. On her guard, she allowed her eyes to scan the few pedestrians and cars that were parked in front of the hotel. Satisfied her surroundings posed no imminent threat she crossed the street and positioned herself behind the steering wheel of the low-cost rental car they had hired upon their arrival. The GPS app's screen popped open on her mobile phone and she clicked on the coordinates her father had sent her. Lars Beeck's address wasn't known to the ordinary man on the street. His covert work had forced him to implement several security measures to keep him safe.

Originally from The Hague, he had started his career as a forensic art investigator in a reputable insurance firm where her parents had met him during a symposium at The British Museum many years back. But it wasn't long before his ability to help solve high profile art crime cases, earned him a reputation as an expert, and just about every and any government security agency worldwide wanted to employ him. When the opportunity presented itself he joined the FBI where he had spent the bulk of his career until he went into retirement five years earlier. Armed with decades of expertise in the art and antiquities field he now spent his retirement contracting his services out to private art dealers, fraud investigators and covert government crime fighting teams across the world. Equipped with the world's best forensic technology and scientific research tools, Alex couldn't ask for anyone better suited to tell her more about the piece of jewelry in her pocket, and what's more, she knew she could trust him to keep their meeting confidential. It was the very nature upon which he ran his clandestine business.

T he red balloon icon on her mobile showed their meeting point northeast from her current location. It would take her just under thirty minutes to get to where she'd been told to wait for further instructions. The mid-morning sun lay hidden behind thick dark clouds that hinted she was to expect heavy downpours very soon but she couldn't help but feel somewhat excited about the imminent meeting with the world renowned Lars Beeck, whom she'd ever only heard about through the grapevine of a few of her insurance company clients. Even when her father had suggested him, he'd been very tightlipped about Lars. She caught herself smiling at her good fortune as her heart skipped another beat. Brought back to reality by the sudden bleep on her mobile phone, she followed its instruction and took a right turn onto a narrow rural road that wound its way between two large olive groves that seemed to continue on forever. With no car, animal, or human in sight for miles she continued to glance at the map that indicated she'd need to travel another five miles along the road down into a valley. As she followed the winding road that gradually transformed into a long steep downhill into the valley, the few rays of sun disappeared behind a blanket of black clouds and moments later, heavy rain poured down onto her windshield. The steady downpour sent her windscreen washers into overdrive bringing little relief to her inability to see the road in front of her. The rental car increased speed as it carried her down the hill and she took her foot off the gas to slow it down. With the window washers now at full speed under the bucketing rain, visibility was down to only a few feet in front of the car. She'd have to stop and wait for the rain to ease, she thought. Alex glanced at the clock on the dashboard. There was no way of contacting Lars if she missed their agreed check-in time at the marker. Deciding she couldn't stop she pushed on. As the car's wheels increased momentum down the hill, Alex slammed on the brakes but found the pedal under her foot offered zero resistance. She pushed the ball of her foot down again but the result was the same. The car rolled faster down the hill and sent panic through her body. She pumped the brakes again, over and over. The brakes weren't working. Deciding her only other option was to use the emergency brake she yanked it back. It also failed. With her body stiff behind the wheel of the car, her hands gripped the steering as she fought hard to keep the vehicle on the road that had all but completely disappeared in front of her. She slammed both feet on the brake pedal again even though she full well knew the result. The speedometer's red numbers increased with every second as the car sped down the hill. Dread flooded her insides while she struggled to control the assemblage of emotions that warred against each other. She lifted her mobile phone from where she had secured it between her thighs and double-tapped the screen with her thumb to enlarge the map. Fear lodged in her throat at the sight of the sharp turn in the road that would send her over the road's edge into the olive grove below if she missed it. Jolted into clarity by the prospect of certain death, she stuck her phone behind her waistband and opened the door as she readied herself to jump out of the car. But it was too late and the momentary weightless feeling of the car floating through the air told her it had already veered off the cliff. As the rain hit her face through the open door she jumped nevertheless, pushing her body away from the airborne car. Having no control over her body, her shoulder slammed hard onto the ground before she bounced and tumbled several times against trees and shrubs. Powerless against the earth's forces to direct the movement of her body, the sudden inability to breathe told her she had collided with something large enough to interrupt her propulsion and bring her body to a forceful halt.

With the wind knocked out of her Alex gasped in an attempt to force air back into her lungs. The continued downpour left her body drenched and as she lay flat on her back struggling to breathe, water collected in her mouth. In a desperate effort not to drown, she managed to turn her head sideways as she forced the water out with her tongue; a fraction of time before her diaphragm released its spasm and her lungs filled with air. Her body reacted to the droplets of water that involuntarily got sucked into her lungs as she coughed into the muddy ground beneath her chin. Sharp bursts of pain soared through her body from her shoulder. It must have dislocated in the fall, she realized. When she managed to use her other arm to push her body up from the muddy pool she was now lying in, her arm instinctively held her ribcage and she found herself gasping for air again, this time as a result of the pain. Now on her knees, gripping her limp arm with the other hand, she lifted her head to take in her surrounds. From where she was knelt between hundreds of large olive trees all around her the car was nowhere to be seen. She turned her face up towards the dark sky and allowed the rain to wash the mud from her eyes and mouth. As she knelt in the olive grove with the cool rainwater washing over her face, she knew her failing brakes were no accident. Someone wanted her dead.

Her hand closed in a fist over the spot on her jacket where she had placed the ring in a hidden inside pocket and let out an audible sigh of relief when it pushed back hard against the palm of her hand.

She reached for her mobile phone where she had stuck it in her waistband. It was gone. Again she fought to keep her head as she realized she'd have no way of finding the meeting point without it. With her one usable arm she wiped the rain from her eyes and scanned the ground directly around her. Increasing the peripheral area from her starting point outwards she managed to stand and continued the search for her phone between the trees. Having finally caught her bearings she set off up the cliff towards the road, groaning with the pain of her injury as she did so, all the while still keeping an eye out for her phone. Her feet disappeared beneath the mud with each labored step, which put additional strain on her ability to climb up the slippery surface. Finding it harder to breathe she paused under a nearby olive tree that stood about thirty feet tall; its foliage bringing her a momentary welcome relief from the relentless rain. She allowed herself a brief moment to rest and as she wiped her eyes again, she heard the dull pinging sound made by the GPS somewhere to her right. Her heart skipped a beat as she listened. There it was again. It took a few paces around the tree before she spotted her phone lying snugly between the branches of an olive tree. She snatched it from between the thick foliage, and cringed with pain when she forgot about her dislocated shoulder. With her cell phone now safely in hand she watched as the map adjusted and the red balloon pulsed in the image. She wasn't that far away. She could walk there, and if she used her accident to her advantage and cut across the valley through the grove, she'd get there on time.

CHAPTER 12

A lex looked at the clock on her phone. She was only a few minutes late and somehow she had managed to make it to the coordinates of the location in one piece. The rain had thankfully stopped but the pain in her shoulder had worsened. Clutching her limp arm closely against her ribcage she waited. What for, she didn't know. She had been standing in the middle of a crop field with nothing and no one in sight for several minutes now. Sudden doubts flooded her mind. She was late, and if Lars Beeck's operation was as slick as she had been told, it was entirely possible he had dismissed her and their meeting. She dropped her head, partly in embarrassment but also in defeat. She closed the map on her phone and clicked the coordinates her father had sent her again. The red balloon marker confirmed she was indeed in the right place. Deciding she had clearly missed the opportunity, she turned to walk back in the direction she had come from but stopped dead in her tracks when her phone suddenly buzzed. It was an instruction. *Walk fifty paces southwest.* Revived with a newfound excitement in the knowledge that she hadn't messed up her chances, she turned and counted out the instruction sent to her. When she arrived at the spot, her eyes scanned over the leaves of the plants that continued to surround her. She looked down at her phone expecting another instruction, but there was none. She turned three hundred and sixty degrees and searched the area around her until her eye caught sight of a plant that appeared ever so slightly greener than the rest in the field. It was about five feet away. With her injury impeding her mobility it was entirely possible she had misjudged her paces. She rushed towards the plant and touched it, and was excited to find it was artificial. Her hand slid down the stem to where it disappeared into a hole camouflaged by artificial soil. The thought crossed her mind that perhaps it was a lever of some sort so she yanked the plant upward. A hollow clicking noise sounded through the air followed by the rustling of leaves to her right and she watched the ground give way to a small manhole between the plants next to her.

"Unbelievable," she said out loud as she gaped down into the space beneath the crop field to where a narrow, curved, spiral staircase greeted her.

Feeling every bit like Alice in Wonderland, Alex descended the staircase that lit up the instant she took her first step. When her foot left the last step at the bottom of the staircase the hatch closed above her head and a long, illuminated, concrete corridor indicated her way forward. Electricity flowed freely through her veins as she ventured into the unknown. Above her head a closed-circuit camera whirred as it followed her movement down the passage to where she stopped in front of a polished silver door resembling that of an elevator's. Two more cameras zoomed in above her head before a mechanical click opened the door.

A short bald man wearing brown tinted Wayfarer reading glasses and an oversized military green safari jacket appeared from behind the door.

"You were but a distant dream when I last had the pleasure of your parents' company." Lars welcomed her in poetic prose.

"I'm sorry I was late," Alex apologized.

"Your courage and tenacity were astounding. I didn't think you'd make it through the grove let alone find your way here. Let me look at your shoulder."

Lars' words left Alex puzzled.

"You know about the... how do you know about the accident? And my shoulder?" she stuttered.

"Fear not, my dear Alexandra. I have eyes in the sky. A simple precautionary measure I take with all my visitors." He flashed a charming smile.

Lars Beeck wasn't at all the intimidating art aficionado she had expected. Instead he was warm, friendly, and slightly on the quirky side. If she had met him in a street café she'd have taken him to be a wildlife photographer. She allowed him to slip her jacket off her injured shoulder before she sat on the solitary wooden stool that he had pulled away from an easel a few feet away. Her eyes took in the underground bunker that looked nothing like one would expect to see buried twenty feet beneath a crop field on the outskirts of Jerusalem. It was instead homely and bright as if daylight somehow managed to find its way in beneath the earth. Tastefully decorated with antique wood and leather furniture it resembled a luxurious apartment in the center of Amsterdam; complete with murals of fake windows showing expansive canal views. In the background, light classical music danced off the warm maple wood-paneled walls where several original art paintings finished off the space. In the furthest corner, a closed door led to the research laboratory that was visible by means of a large square glass window in the wall.

Alex winced as Lars attempted to move and lift her arm.

"My apologies, but it had to be done. Your shoulder is without a doubt dislocated. I'll have it back in place in no time."

"That's not necessary, thank you. My husband has a medical background. I'm sure he'll fix it when I get back to the—" Alex interrupted herself with an ear-splitting yell when Lars, without any warning, yanked her arm back into the socket.

"There, as good as new. I'll get some ice."

Still in shock from the unsolicited medical care, Alex watched as Lars glided in a mono waltz across the oak floors to the three-beat rhythm of Johann Strauss's famous *Blue Danube*. She gently moved her arm, rolling her shoulder to find that he had indeed managed to manipulate it back into place.

"Ice and something for the inflammation. Drink up," Lars popped two capsules and a glass of water into her hand.

"How did you know how to do that?" she asked.

"Oh, just a nifty little trick my chiropractor taught me many years ago. I have a pesky rotator cuff from spending too much time on the tennis court when I was once young and carefree. The problem is, it never really goes away, so I have to keep an eye on it. Now, what is it that brings you to my humble abode?"

Alex reached for the ring in her jacket and dropped it in his hand.

"We found this in a Second Temple period burial site."

"Be still my beating heart!"

Alex didn't have to say more. The expression of surprise on his face betrayed that he knew exactly what she had brought him.

"You recognize it?" she said.

"If not for physically holding it between my fingers I would've believed it to be nothing more than ancient lore. I never thought I'd see the day," Lars continued in shock.

"What do you know?" Alex probed.

"You're looking at an almost two-thousand-year-old seal ring, and if I'm right, it belonged to a high priest."

"I suspect you're right. We found an ossuary marked Joseph, son of Caiaphas there too. I had to make an anonymous donation to the museum so as not to jeopardize our mission. They're running tests as we speak so we should know if it's his remains any day now. I wasn't sure if they were linked but I guess now I know."

Alex followed Lars to where he had spun around and darted into his research lab the moment the words had left her lips. As if he was late for an appointment he pulled a book from a floor-to-ceiling bookshelf in the far corner of the room and hastily flipped through the pages.

"Here!" he exclaimed as he stuck the book under her nose. "This is a sketch of a similar ring that was found almost twenty-three years ago in Crete. The inscription reads—"

"Joseph, son of Caiaphas," Alex read the words on his behalf.

"It was speculated that this was one of two rings, since most high priests kept one in their stately home while they wore the other one. But they never found the second one," Lars continued with excitement.

"Why Crete of all places? I thought he lived here, in Jerusalem."

"He did, except no one really knows where or how he died. There are a few different theories about Caiaphas' death. One of which is based on Jesus' prophecy at the time of His hearing, as is recorded in Mark 14:61–61 when Jesus said, *'and you will see the Son of Man... coming on the clouds of heaven.'* Then, in Acts 8:57, after His resurrection, it was recorded that Caiaphas might have seen Jesus sitting on the right hand of God so that would indicate he was still alive at that time. *The Apostolic Constitutions* of the late fourth century show a record or a church tradition in which it's said that Caiaphas killed himself, possibly as a result of guilt and shame. But then in the *Letter of Tiberius to Pilate* it is recorded that Caiaphas, Pilate and other Jewish rulers were arrested on the orders of Tiberius and then taken to Rome. On the way, however, Caiaphas died in Crete, and since the 'earth would not receive his body,' he was covered with a cairn of stones. Up until the nineteenth century there was a site known as the tomb of Caiaphas near the Crete city of Knossos."

Lars slammed the book closed and placed it back in its place on the shelf. With the ring now on his index finger, he pulled an apron over his head and took up position behind a high-tech microscope. Enlarged images of the ring flashed on a large computer monitor in front of him as he inspected the piece of silver jewelry. Alex watched silently from where she stood behind him, intrigued by the low, short, guttural sounds he made every few seconds. Without warning he flew off his chair and snatched the book back off the shelf, hurriedly flipping back to the sketch as he walked over to his workbench.

"Well, what do you know?" he finally said.

"What?"

"At first glance it looks identical, but then, there's this." Lars pointed to two symbols on the matrix.

"What are we looking at?" Alex asked.

"Something remarkable if I'm correct. We know ancient Christians had a deep appreciation for symbols and their power. These seals, along with ancient scrolls, are evidence of that. Each symbol represented something and, as is the case here, one stamp like this told an entire story. Now usually, priests would have their family symbol and history et cetera at the time of it being used. But look at the first ring that was found. What do you see?"

"I see a symbol looking like the letter P."

"And now look at this one."

"I see two additional symbols. The alpha and omega letters together and one that looks like a childlike sketch of a fish," Alex answered.

"Precisely. Neither of these two images was used before the crucifixion; not in the early days of Christianity."

"So what do you make of it?"

"The letter P is in fact the staurogram, or tau-rho as in the Greek *tau*, the letter T, and *rho*, the letter P. Together they represent the Greek word for *cross*. The first and last letters of the Greek alphabet, as we know, represent the Alpha and the Omega as mentioned in the book of Revelation when Christ referred to Himself as the *First and the Last, the Beginning and the End*. Putting the two together like this represents the eternity of Christ as the Son of God. Which then brings us to the final symbol, the fish, or *ichthus*, which is the Greek word for fish. This was one of the most important early Christian symbols. Not only did fish feature in miracles throughout the first four books of the New Testament, known as the Gospels, but the *ichthus* was taken as an acrostic for the Greek phrase 'Iēsous Christos Theou Hyios Sōtēr', which means 'Jesus Christ, Son of God Savior.' So, considering these rings both belonged to Caiaphas, the very man who plotted to have Jesus Christ crucified, doesn't it seem odd that he would make these proclamations?" Lars asked Alex.

Alex found herself staring at the magnified image on the screen.

"You're right, it does seem odd, except I don't know what to make of it," she confessed.

"Oh, but you will. It will all fall into place in a moment."

More perplexed than ever, Alex watched as Lars worked his way through detailed sketches and computer drawings. His enthusiasm was electrifying.

"Not to interrupt your arts and crafts but what are you doing?" she eventually asked with a twisted smile when she couldn't hide her curiosity anymore.

"I am recreating the original ring. If my hunch is correct, you're about to unlock a mystery this world has never seen!"

CHAPTER 13

For the next hour Alex watched as Lars set about drafting the original seal ring on paper after which he fed the images into a computer program. It wasn't long before the near silent humming of a 3D printer echoed through the room and Alex found herself staring at a near perfect replica of the first of the two seal rings found twenty-three years earlier.

"It's not quite the real thing, but it will certainly do the trick," Lars said with even more excitement than before as he moved back behind his table.

"That looks great but now what?" she asked.

"Now we have to decode it," he answered.

"Decode it? What do you mean?"

Lars didn't answer her. Instead he had already started melting blobs of wax onto a clear glass sheet after which he took each ring and pressed the stamps firmly into the wax. Alex didn't push him. Instead, she allowed him to continue in silence while she scanned over the samples he'd discarded. It was clear he had closed himself off from her while conducting some kind of experiment.

When Lars finally got up and backed away from his table, scratching the back of his head in confusion, Alex spoke again.

"Perhaps I can help somehow if you tell me what you're experimenting with."

"I honestly thought it would work," he said.

"What? Tell me what's going on," Alex pushed.

"The code, we need to crack the code," he said again, hardly making any sense.

"Okay, you're not making any sense. What's going on, Lars?"

Lars flew across the floor and exited the lab, all the while still scratching his head. Alex didn't follow him. Instead she picked up both rings and slipped one on each of her index fingers.

"What if you're wrong?" she yelled at him from inside the lab and walked over to where he had pressed the stamps into the wax.

Moments later, Lars was next to her.

"About what exactly? I'm telling you there's a hidden message in the rings," he said, looking puzzled. He was a humble man but he was rarely wrong when it came to his work.

"What if Caiaphas wore both rings, simultaneously?"

Lars watched as Alex stretched both her hands out in front of her staring at the two rings on her hands.

"Why would he do that? It would entirely defeat the purpose."

"Precisely," Alex confirmed.

"Okay now you're not making sense, Alex."

"Think about it. If the normal practice for a high priest were to keep one ring in his home while he had the other in his possession for when he traveled, wouldn't the rings be identical? Yet, these aren't. They couldn't be more different from each other. Not only are they different, you mentioned that some of these images only came into existence *after* the crucifixion."

Alex kept quiet as she waited for Lars' mind to catch up to hers.

"They weren't the official seal rings," he concluded while the corners of his mouth turned up into a wide grin that exposed all his teeth.

Alex smiled back. "I think he wore both, like jewelry."

Lars started pacing the room, his fingertips webbed out and joined together in front of his chest as he worked out a theory.

"Well, let's play this out according to what we know from the scriptures. After Jesus Christ was resurrected and performed miracles all over Israel in the living flesh, and the people saw what Caiaphas had done, he was ostracized. It's said he took his family and went into hiding. He continued to wear his official clothing, which could've included the rings. Only everyone thought nothing of it and just assumed they were his seal rings, a reminder of the position he once held, so to speak."

"Except they weren't. They couldn't have been because they're not identical," Alex added.

Lars leaped across the room and took hold of Alex's hands, grinning from ear to ear.

"I'm right aren't I? There's a message hidden in these rings. There has to be."

Alex nodded. Her entire body was tingling with the prospect that they might be onto something far more important than what two ancient rings declared at face value.

"That would certainly explain a whole lot," she said. "Like why someone would kill over it," she added.

"Wait, someone died because of this ring."

Alex nodded. "Yes, a young student who came here with his best friend on holiday. They accidentally discovered the ring in the Peace Forest while out on a sightseeing tour. The next thing they knew someone who eventually caught up with them was chasing them and killed one of them. The other has been on the run since then. He's currently in custody for questioning, presumably on suspicion of murdering his best friend."

Lars walked the width of the laboratory again, staring at his feet as he did so.

"Someone tried to kill you too," he said. "How did they know you had the ring?"

Alex shrugged her shoulders. "I'm one of only six people who knew we had the ring and I know my team wouldn't have said anything to anyone outside our group. That leaves Luke, the other student. We strongly suspect he and his friend must have told someone about the ring when they first found it, but he hasn't been in contact with anyone since we saved him from some wannabe kidnappers who might have thought they could exploit his family. They couldn't have known about the ring since we found Luke with it still in his possession. No one knew. Unless..."

Alex went quiet as the penny dropped. She pulled her mobile phone from her jacket pocket and began to dial Sam's number.

"There's no signal," she said slightly panicked.

"Yes, sorry, I jam any external satellite signals. For security reasons, that's all. You can use this phone, it's a secure line... untraceable." He handed her a cell phone.

Alex dialed Sam's number again. He didn't answer. She dialed it again and when he didn't answer the second time either, she dialed Matt whose voice sounded on the other side a mere second after it rang.

"Sheila, you're late," Matt went off at her.

"Where's Sam?"

"He and Ronita aren't back yet. I thought we agreed you'd all be back here an hour ago."

"Matt, listen to me. Ravid is in on it. Whatever's going on here, he's in on it."

"He's the police working this case with us, Alex."

"Yes, and he's not wanted us on this case since the moment you met him. Look, I'll explain later but for now you need to find Sam and Ronita and get them to safety. Their lives might be in danger. The brakes on my car were cut and I nearly ended up off a cliff. Actually the car did go off the cliff. But that's beside the point. I'm with my contact so I'm safe for now, but I think we're onto something. I'll make my way back shortly. Just find Sam!"

Alex dropped the phone back onto Lars's desk, pulled both rings off her fingers and placed them side by side on the counter in front of him.

"We don't have much time, Lars. We need to figure this thing out. Starting with what happened to the first ring that was found more than twenty years ago."

"No one knows. It vanished and has been missing ever since its discovery. And up until now, the prospect of there even being a second ring has been nothing but an ancient myth."

Alex stared at the two rings, studying the images on each up close.

"That's it!" Alex exclaimed. "Whoever took the first ring must be who's after this one. Somehow word got out about it and they've been after it since. If you're right in thinking there's a hidden code in this ring, then we have to find and decipher it before they catch up to us."

Lars's face lit up.

"What?" Alex asked curiously when Lars folded his arms and smiled as if he'd just uncovered a secret she knew nothing about.

"For more than two decades the art world has been silent about the first discovery. It was found, went missing, and no one talked about it much again. Now the second ring is discovered and a person lands up dead because of it.

There's a connection. Apart from an obvious one." His smile returned baiting Alex to guess what he'd already figured out.

Alex turned, her hands on her hips as she worked through the riddle in her head.

"They're only worth something when they work together! Like the alpha and omega emblem. The code doesn't just lie in this ring. It lies in combining both rings!" Alex cried out in excitement.

Lars touched his nose with his forefinger. "You got it. I've been looking at this entirely wrong."

Newfound excitement flooded their arteries as the pair set about inspecting the images on the rings but when, an hour later, they were nowhere closer to finding the code, Alex stepped away from the counter where a multitude of sketches lay scattered all over it.

"We're missing something, Lars. There's nothing out of the ordinary here. It's just a bunch of pictures that tell a story that's not making any sense."

Alex poured herself a glass of water and after taking a drink, placed the glass next to the images on the counter. The bright light from the nearby overhead lamp pierced through the glass onto one of the images in the second ring reversing it onto the counter behind it. As her mind digested what was transforming right in front of her eyes, she snatched the rings up between her fingers. Lars watched as Alex moved the rings into position to where the light cast mirror images through the glass of water. As she turned and twisted the rings in the bright light from the lamp and reflected the reversed images in both the rings onto one of the sheets of paper, the clear outlines of a map slowly became visible.

CHAPTER 14

Alex walked into the foyer of the hotel after Lars had dropped her off at the front entrance. He had insisted on driving her back himself saying her father would never forgive him if he didn't make sure she got back safely. Her heart beat faster with each step she took as she headed up to the room. But as excited as she was to share the news about her and Lars' discovery, she couldn't help feeling anxious over Sam. She'd almost been killed earlier that day and if her theory were correct his life and the entire team's lives would be in danger too. The elevator ride dragged on and once its doors opened, she found herself striding down the corridor towards the room. Ready to face whatever came her way she burst through the hotel room's door desperate to see Sam alive and well.

"I was worried sick about you!" Sam's warm voice filled her ears.

Alex threw her arms around her husband's neck. "Me too."

"Glad you made it back safely, Sheila. Romeo here forced the truth about your failing brakes out of me," Matt said.

"That was hardly a brake failure now was it? It's a brand-new rental. What happened?" Sam asked, still looking concerned.

"I'm fine, don't worry. Wait until I show you what we discovered!" Alex said, bursting to tell them.

"We have some news of our own," Ronita said from where she sat working on her laptop.

"You first then," Alex offered, seeing the saddened look in her eyes.

"Luke is dead. Somehow, I guess he thought suicide was his only option. I never saw that coming though," Sam informed her.

"That makes perfect sense," Alex said, sounding more like she'd found another piece of the puzzle rather than being sympathetic.

"Luke killing himself makes sense? That seems a bit heart-less, don't you think? I thought you liked the guy," Ronita spoke her mind in surprise to Alex's reaction, or lack thereof.

"Something tells me you're not surprised to hear that at all. You expected as much, didn't you?" Sam read his wife's familiar body language.

"Unfortunately, yes. I think we are all a target. Luke didn't commit suicide. I'll bet my life on it," Alex said as she helped herself to a cola from the minibar.

"He hanged himself, Alex. Sam and I saw him with our own eyes. There was a note and everything," Ronita said defensively.

"Was that before or after you had a chance to speak to him? Let me guess, before right?" Alex answered her own question and watched as Ronita confirmed it with a slight nod of the head.

"How did you know?" Ronita asked.

"They made it look like a suicide because Ravid and most likely some of his men are in on it. They killed him before he could talk."

"And there it is," Matt said, leaning his shoulder against the wall. I thought you were just spitting theories on the phone."

"Who apart from the five of us knew about the ring?" Alex asked the group.

"Just us, Luke and Nathan," Ronita answered.

"Correct, but Nathan's been dead for a while, so that left us and Luke. We know he and Nathan must have told someone after they had first found the ring since Nathan ended up dead to begin with. But Luke's been with us the entire time since we saved him from the contractors. No one knew we had found him. He also never left our side so no one else could possibly know he had given us the ring." Alex paused.

"Luke must have told Ravid when they questioned him then," Ronita said.

"Precisely. Before you could see him," Alex continued.

"And then he ends up dead and your brakes get cut." Sam put the final piece of the puzzle together.

Matt walked to the window and stared out into the streets below.

"You're right. He's had eyes on us the whole time. The night in the cemetery, how did he know we were there? Red had jammed the cameras and we had already taken the guards down, yet he arrived out of thin air and placed Luke in custody." Matt unpicked the events.

"Which brings us to what you and your dad's contact found," Sam added.

"We found a second ring." Alex took both replica rings from her pocket and placed them side by side on the table in front of them.

"That's what you're so excited about. A plastic ring that looks as if it came from a kid's cereal packet?" Matt queried.

"Actually it's made from polylactic acid, otherwise known as PLA, and yes, it's a near perfect replica of a ring found about twenty-three years ago, and this is a 3D printed model. It went missing almost immediately after it was discovered. Guess what was inscribed on it."

"Joseph, son of Caiaphas," Red blurted out before he continued. "She's right. It says here it's never been found and that it was speculated to be one of two rings belonging to Caiaphas." He confirmed her statement from where he had already researched it on the Internet.

"Okay, we still haven't figured out why someone would want to kill over our ring, let alone one that went missing more than twenty years ago," Matt said.

The small team watched as Alex emptied a bottle of water into a glass and placed the two rings on the paper just as they had been in Lars' laboratory. When her torchlight cast the mirrored shadows onto the paper from behind the glass, she paused and forced all eyes onto the image. Matt shrugged his shoulders and raised his eyebrows to hint he didn't quite discern her demonstration but Alex smiled and watched his face as she turned the rings into position. As the outlines of the map appeared she was convinced they all stopped breathing simultaneously.

"It's a hidden treasure map!" Red was the first to express his excitement, which was soon followed by Ronita's, "No way!"

"Well, it's something all right. I can't call it a treasure map just yet, but it's something," Alex said.

"I have the coolest computer program fresh off the FBI tech shelves that I've been dying to try out. I'll scan the image and see if I can match it to any particular location. If it exists, this program will find it," Red said, rubbing his palms together with excitement before his fingers pounded the computer keys.

"Sounds like we're getting somewhere then," Ronita commented. "What do we do about Ravid?" she continued.

"Nothing. Not a word to anyone at this stage. We cannot let him know we suspect he's dirty. Got it?" Matt said sternly.

"So we're just going to let him get away with murder?" Ronita challenged her boss.

"Yes," he answered.

"He murdered Luke and possibly Nathan too. Not to mention that he almost killed Alex as well. We can't just leave it. We have to arrest him," Ronita continued, visibly upset by the betrayal.

"Based on what, Ronita? If we're going to take a police official down in his own city we'd better have gathered concrete evidence to prove our allegations first. We're all on the same page here. He should be locked up, but we have to do this correctly from the onset or he'll walk away scot-free. We need hard evidence that will stick in court before we set off to challenge a foreign government," Matt said.

Red's voice cut across the small room.

"Oh that reminds me, boss. Ronnie and I got some great intel on our upstanding detective. Some of his files were classified. Weird right? I cracked them though and I found a few things that I think you'll find very interesting."

Red flashed their findings on the big screen for the team to see.

"He's been the chief detective for a number of years and several of his past cases were dismissed for the same reasons: 'lack of evidence'. What's interesting is that it's the same perps whose names keep popping up in every single one of those cases. Different crimes, different cases but the same criminals. And the common denominator is that Ravid was the chief detective on each case. The witnesses disappear into thin air or retract their statements and the evidence vanished from the evidence rooms."

"What's the timeline on the cases? Any pattern there?" Matt asked.

Ronita's fingers danced over her keyboard.

"Interesting. The crimes are consistent; every month roughly around the same time," Ronita reported.

"And let me guess. It mostly involves theft and arms possession," Matt said.

"Yes. How did you know?" Ronita asked.

"I think I've just figured out what our detective is up to. Weapons trade," Matt announced.

"You're saying they're smuggling weapons out of the country?" Alex verified her understanding.

"Not out, in," Sam corrected.

"That's what they were trying to bury in the graveyard. They weren't looking for anything, they were digging the holes to hide their weapons," Alex pieced it together.

"Except we disrupted their operation which is why Ravid got there in such a hurry. Nice work, guys. Let's see if we can connect him to any local trafficking groups. If he's getting weapons into the country he's trading them for something and speaking from experience, I'm pretty certain it's antiquities. Work your magic, Ronnie, and find out if there's a connection between our Syrian friends from the graveyard and Ravid. They could be paying him off to turn a blind eye or he could be running the operation. If he's clever he'd be operating under an alias so use his face when you search," Matt instructed.

"Copy that, boss, and sorry for before. I just don't like crooked cops," Ronita apologized.

"If my suspicions are correct we have bigger fish to fry, Ronnie. I have a feeling Ravid is nothing more than a pawn in this game. We'll find the head of the snake and when we do, they'll all go down," Matt said.

CHAPTER 15

In light of their suspicions the team remained in HQ and focused their attention on interpreting the map. Red's computer program had been running the outline for several hours without any positive results.

"I thought you said this new tech's supposed to be off the charts." Matt leaned in over Red's shoulder.

"That's what I was told, yes. It's scanning through millions of possible variants across cities, countries, islands and just about any geographical location known to man. The entire world is in DotGrid format inside this program," Red explained.

"I have no idea what that means but what logic tells me is that this could take days, Red. We don't have days. Someone out there understands the value of this ring and we now know they forced Luke into telling them that we have it." Matt's usually optimistic outlook had turned to concern.

"Then why haven't they broken down our door yet?" Ronita asked.

"Because they're waiting for us to decipher it. We're being watched, and the moment we leave this hotel they'll be following us," Alex said from where she stood at the window and stared at the parked surveillance vehicle in the street below.

"Well, we're nowhere close to finding out what that outline is. It looks like an area map but there's no 'X' marks the spot or names of any kind on there. It could literally be an outline of an animal for all we know," Sam commented.

"You're right. We're assuming it's a map. We should explore other possibilities too," Alex suggested as she walked to where the two rings lay on the table.

"Do we know what these symbols mean?" Matt asked as he sat down at the table next to her.

"For the most part, yes. They're Greek symbols that translate into words or phrases. The first ring is different from the second in that it only has the tao-rho on it—the Greek letters, meaning *cross*. The second ring has two more symbols added—the alpha omega and the ichthus. Combined it translates to 'Jesus Christ Son of God'. The same message is essentially repeated in all three images," Alex explained.

"I thought you said this man hated God," Matt queried.

"Not God; he was a priest who served his version of God. He hated the man who said He was God's son," Sam corrected him.

"So why did he have rings claiming that Jesus was the Son of God? This contradiction as much as admitted it. That doesn't make sense," Matt said.

Alex stared at the rings on the table.

"It's a confession! He's confessing it," Alex jumped up in excitement.

"A confession to what? He was a high priest long before the crucifixion. I thought you said these were his rings," Ronita said.

"They were, but they were crafted *after* the crucifixion. These symbols didn't even exist before the crucifixion. The tao-rho for example was one of the earliest Christian images of the crucifixion. That's how they recorded events, through symbols. The Egyptians did it centuries before the time. It's throughout the entire Old Testament," Alex explained.

"You're not making sense, Alex. What does that have to do with a confession?" Matt said.

"He confessed his sin and that he was wrong. It's an acknowledgement of what he had done," Sam said, casting a proud smile at Alex.

"I really want to say I understand what you're trying to explain here, but you two geniuses lost me," Matt said, throwing his hands in the air.

"It's so obvious, boss. The rings are his personal journal. The symbols translate into him mentioning the crucifixion and that he admits the truth. Jesus was resurrected and went on to live forty more days performing dozens of miracles. How could Caiaphas not believe He was the Son of God after he personally saw Him dying on the cross and then buried only to see Jesus walking in the flesh all around him?" Ronita's explanation brought the room to silence with Matt staring at her as if she were a stranger.

"What? I was curious to know who this Caiaphas guy was so I read all four of the Gospels last night. It's all there in the Bible," she defended.

"Well since you put it that way..." Matt joked still not fully understanding Alex's theory.

"Look, Ronita's right. It's exactly like a journal in which he made a confession. It's my understanding that there are several theories based around his death. Some say he was apparently guilt-ridden about what he had done and decided to kill himself. Others claim he was ostracized, fled, and went into hiding where he died a lonely man. Another hypothesis is that he was captured and arrested on the orders of Tiberius who then transported him to Rome. Except he died on the way there in..."

Alex suddenly paused midway.

"Wait! Red, are you able to centralize your search criteria to one country?" Alex said with enthusiasm.

"Absolutely. I can isolate it right down to a city if you need me to."

"Yes, perfect! Run a search on Crete," Alex instructed.

"As in the Greek island?" Matt verified.

Alex fervently paced the room and shook her hands like an excited child who couldn't get his story out fast enough would do.

"No one knows exactly how and where Caiaphas died but one theory around his death is that he died in Crete. That's where the first ring was discovered twenty-three years ago. These symbols are all Greek, so if our theory is correct in that it was a depiction of his confession, it's safe to assume he had the rings on him when he died," Alex spoke her thinking process out loud.

"Then how did the second ring make it back here?" Matt asked.

"I don't know. All I know is that back then, during the first century, people were buried with certain items they thought they might need in the afterlife. It makes sense then that his rings would have been buried with him," Alex said.

"Well, we found his remains in the ossuary and the second ring nearby. Could his remains have been moved from Crete back to Jerusalem?" Sam theorized.

"I suppose it's possible, yes. I guess we'll never truly know all the mysteries of the Bible," said Alex, "but I do know that we have a concrete lead that we need to follow up on. This ring means something to someone who is very prepared to kill us for it, and we need to know why."

"He was rich wasn't he? Didn't you say high priests were very wealthy back then?" Matt asked.

Ronita jumped up from where she'd quietly been listening to their hypothesis, sporting a smile so wide it looked as if her face would split in two.

"Are you saying what I think you're saying? This is a treasure hunt, for a two-thousand-year-old lost treasure!"

"Whoa now, calm down. No one said anything about a lost treasure," Matt said while he grabbed a bottle of water from the nearby kitchenette.

"I wouldn't be so sure, Matt. Ancient lost treasures do exist. We should know, but, Ronita, I suppose it depends on what you'd call a treasure to begin with. Not every *treasure* translates to gold coins and jewelry," Alex smiled. "The truth is we don't know what significance these two rings hold. It might be nothing at all."

"Or not!" Ronita held fast to the exciting prospect.

"All we have are theories based on assumptions at this stage. I think all our intel is random and purely circumstantial. Not to mention I'm still staring down the barrel of an alleged illegal weapons trade and two murders. None of this connects to any of the real reasons we're all here. We're grasping at invisible straws," Matt said, sounding frustrated and doubtful.

"I agree with you, Matt. Something doesn't quite sit right with me," Sam assured him. "We're missing something."

"Or someone! Our exemplary detective is guilty as sin! His face is plastered all over Facebook," Red yelled from behind his screens.

"And? It's Facebook. Everyone's on Facebook," Matt prompted.

"And it's not attached to his real name," Red added as he shared his findings to the big screen. "Your hunch was spot-on, boss. He's definitely involved with our Syrian friends. They're all connected to a Facebook group page called *Muharibu Alhuriya*, Arabic meaning 'Freedom Fighters'. Ravid's known only as *The Watchman*. The page has thousands of pictures of looted antiquities. Everything from Roman mosaics to full Pharaonical coffins, and everything in between. Many of these relics are listed on the Bible Lands Museum's *Finds Gone Astray* list. And thanks to Facebook's fantastic algorithms, there are now several similar extremist groups cropping up on my suggestions list, and Ravid's on quite a few of them."

"Excellent work, Red! Now we're getting somewhere concrete. Can you scan through the photos for our Caiaphas rings?" Matt asked.

"There's nothing even remotely close to the rings," Red reported back after a few minutes.

"What about weapons?" Matt tried again.

"Nothing. Not one single mention of weapons of any kind. They're smart, covering their tracks. My guess is they use the encrypted messaging to communicate details on weapons, trade points etc." Red continued.

"What if you posed as a member? Can you join the group?" Ronita asked.

Red's fingers danced over his keyboard, clicking the mouse every few seconds.

"That's interesting," he finally said, but then continued clicking in silence.

"Well, spit it out, boy," Matt said in a slightly agitated tone.

"As a new member I'm required to pay a tax on any sales generated by my participation."

"So the Facebook Admin is profiting from the trades. He's the middleman," Sam said.

"That's smart. Now what?" Alex said.

Matt paced the room, which suddenly fell quiet, a direct contrast to the earlier excitement over the prospect of a treasure hunt.

"Agree to the fee and post an image of the ring. We'll lure them out of the gutters. Use a loop on our current IP address. If they're this smart there's a good chance they have tech guys in their corner too. I don't want any traces back to us. It's time we found out just how valuable the ring is, and with any luck, it will lead us straight to the head of the snake," Matt said.

CHAPTER 16

With a plan of action and feeling every bit in control of their search, the team executed the risky strategy.

"Okay, we're in, boss. The rugged looking Mr. Smith has cast his net. I guess now we wait for a fish to bite," Red said.

"Mr. Smith, huh? You wish!" Ronita laughed at her colleague.

Matt leaned in over Red's shoulder to scan over his work.

"Perfect. That should shake a few tail feathers and I bet 'The Watchman' will crop up first. Keep a close eye on it but keep working on the Facebook groups and see if you can find out who the Admin is," Matt instructed.

"Will do, boss but Facebook's security is tighter than Fort Knox. Their user identities are impenetrable," Red answered.

"Red, you're the best in the business. If you could hack into the Federal Reserve Bank's main server you can hack into Facebook," Matt said.

"He hacked into the Federal Reserve Bank's mainframe?" a stunned Sam asked in response to the information.

"Sure did. He might only be twenty-three but he's got quite the talent," Matt said proudly as if he spoke of his own son.

"So how did he end up working with you?" Alex asked.

"As smart as he was they eventually caught him. He served eighteen months behind bars and then became a chief informant for the FBI. The next thing I knew my task force included him on my team and now I'm stuck with him." His mischievous smile made it obvious Matt liked Red.

"I'm impressed. The youth of today certainly know all the shortcuts," Sam said.

"Well, while we're clinging onto our wiser youthful years, what do you say we take a quick flight to Crete and see what we can come up with? It's only ninety minutes from here. We should be back in twenty-four hours," Alex suggested.

"Tell you what, I'll stay put here to keep an eye on these two and I'll arrange a helicopter to take you and Sam. Besides, you're going to need a distraction while you slip out the back door. That car hasn't moved down there so I'm pretty certain you'll be followed the instant you set foot onto the curb," Matt said.

"Oh, Hollywood celebrities do it all the time. You and I can dress up to look like Alex and Sam and when we're sure they've followed us out of the area, we'll lose them," Ronita suggested casually.

"Like I said, the youth of today know it all. Let's do it," Sam agreed.

"Any idea where you're going to start your search? Crete might be an island but finding a tomb that might or might not exist is still going to be a needle in a haystack," Matt said.

"Well, as it happens, my contact mentioned Caiaphas was supposedly buried in Knossos which is about two miles south of Heraklion. I'll ask some of the locals to point us in the right direction once we're there," Alex said as she gathered her backpack.

The Hollywood distraction (as the team now fondly referred to it) went down without a hitch and it wasn't long before Alex and Sam made a safe undetected exit to the roof of the hotel where they climbed into the helicopter Matt had arranged for them. The pilot, an American, briefly greeted them and didn't as much as exchange one more sentence with them for most of the trip.

"You're American, right?" Sam tried about halfway into the flight somewhere over the Mediterranean. Sam was seated in the cockpit next to the pilot.

The pilot didn't as much as blink, as if Sam and Alex were invisible.

"I'm Sam and that's my wife, Alex. We're British. How long have you worked in Jerusalem?" He tried again, and watched the pilot's body tense up with each word he spoke.

The pilot ignored Sam's effort to make conversation and instead shot a quick glance at his instrument panel, adjusting a knob overhead. As his arm reached up, Sam spotted the black handle of a gun just about visible on his hip from under his jacket. Making sure not to react Sam caught his breath in his throat and briefly looked back at Alex who was oblivious in the back seat. Looking as calm as was possible on the outside, his mind raced a million miles an hour. Something didn't sit right. The pilot seemed anxious and on edge and suddenly Sam's entire body was on high alert. They were at least forty-five minutes from Crete if his timing was correct. He tried to rationalize why the pilot might be carrying a gun but he couldn't. If his actions had been friendly towards them he wouldn't have been suspicious but the guy had been nothing but evasive and hostile since they left Jerusalem. Sam's suspicions were well served when ten minutes later the pilot pulled his gun and aimed it directly at Sam.

"Get out!" he commanded.

"What are you doing? Have you lost your mind?" Sam overreacted in the hopes of alerting Alex who had fallen asleep behind him. It worked. Her body grew rigid the second her eyes caught sight of the unexpected scene that was unfolding in front of her.

"Don't even think of trying anything," he told Alex.

"Who's paying you?" Alex said bravely.

"None of your business. Now get out, both of you or I'll shoot you!"

"You're not going to shoot him and you know it. I'll have my arm around your throat before you can take your next breath," Alex warned sternly.

"I'd listen to her if I were you. Whoever's paying you to get rid of us we'll double it," Sam chanced.

"No one's paying me, now stop messing with me and get out."

Droplets of sweat trickled over the pilot's brows and emotion lay thick in his eyes.

"They're forcing you, aren't they?" Sam finally pieced it together. "Your body language has been telling me that the entire flight, mate. We can help you. Just tell us who's blackmailing you."

The pilot's eyes confirmed Sam was correct. Filled with fear and paranoia he stared at Sam, nervously moving his gun back and forth between Alex and Sam.

"Trust us, we can help you," Alex urged from behind.

"I can't. They'll kill them if I don't go back with proof. I can't risk it," the man broke down. "Please, just jump. You're not that far from Crete and at this height there might still be a chance you can survive the fall. They're going to kill my family. I don't have a choice," the pilot pleaded.

"You always have a choice, mate. Who's blackmailing you? Tell us and we'll fake the jump so you have your proof," Sam said.

It was clear Sam got through to him when the pilot broke into tears. "I don't know, honestly. I've never spoken to them. I run a clean business but a few hours ago I got this message."

The pilot flashed up a photograph of his wife and two daughters, obviously in captivity.

"Then the phone rang and a computer voice said to pick you up at your hotel's helipad and drop you in the ocean if

I ever want to see my family again. I have to send a video clip of you falling into the ocean back to an email address as proof."

Sam's fingers scrolled through the pilot's call directory in search of the caller's number and copied it onto his own mobile phone.

"Where's the email address you're meant to send proof to?" Alex asked.

"It's there, at the end of the video message."

Sam played the video and Alex watched the pilot gradually lose grip of his emotions as the panicked cries of his young daughters sounded through the phone. With one hand gripping the joystick and his other still pointing the gun at Sam, the pilot suddenly lost control of his emotions and switched the gun's aim at Alex.

"Jump or I'll shoot her! You can't help me and I'm not stupid enough to take the risk. I'll give you three seconds to jump before I kill her!"

"Okay, calm down, mate. What's your name?" Sam tried to reason.

"It doesn't matter what my name is! Just get out!" he shouted louder, losing all grasp on his sanity.

Having now run out of options with a maniac that was threatening to kill his wife, Sam reached for the handle of the door to open it. His hands pushed hard against the force of the air against the door as he stared down into the dark waters about fifteen thousand feet below. He knew full well no one could survive a fall at that altitude. Even if he chanced it and jumped there was a far greater chance he'd hit the rear rotor first.

"Get on with it!" the pilot shouted again.

Sam looked back at Alex where the hysterical pilot's gun still held her captive. His eyes met hers for a brief moment. It was enough to communicate a telepathic message to his wife as they had, for the most part, successfully done all the years they'd worked together. Alex lowered her eyelids in confirmation that she was ready to execute what she had read in Sam's eyes. Sam wedged his foot between his seat and the hinge of the door and in one swift movement, pushed his back against the pilot's arm while Alex used the distraction to disarm their captor. It took all of two seconds to execute and they caught the pilot completely off his guard. The sudden maneuver forced the helicopter out of control and tilted it to one side, throwing the pilot back against his door. He fought hard to gain control over his body as the helicopter continued to spiral out of control. Sam gripped the joystick in an effort to level out the aircraft but the gravitational force was too strong. As the helicopter's momentum changed its direction, the pilot's body flung back and forth until his head slammed against the metal doorframe and his body went flaccid.

"Sam, do something!" Alex shouted in panic as they tumbled toward the unwelcoming ocean, but not even Sam's double-fisted clutch around the joystick was enough to pull the nose of the helicopter back up into position.

"We're not going to make it, Sam!" Alex shouted while her eyes remained fixed on the dark ocean that drew closer by the second.

Knowing there was nothing left to do, Sam let go of the lever and looked back into his wife's eyes the moment the aircraft slammed into the deep waters of the Mediterranean Sea.

CHAPTER 17

The rushing sound of water filled Sam's ears as he struggled to gain control of his body under the sea. His mouth flooded with water and the salt stung his eyes. As his arms pushed against the water his hand hit a hard object that made a piercing sting reverberate up his arm. From the corner of his eye he saw daylight several feet above his head and allowed his body to instinctively turn toward it. His lungs ached for oxygen. Desperate to satisfy its need for air his arms stretched up toward the surface that seemed to move further out of reach the more desperate he got. When his face finally broke through the ocean surface he drew in a deep breath and filled his lungs with oxygen.

"Alex! Alex!" He searched between the swells around him.

Unable to see her over the ocean waves he took a deep breath and stuck his head under the water, feeling the now familiar sting behind his eyeballs again. His eyes frantically searched through the dark shadows of the water, taking note of the helicopter's wreckage as it slowly sank to the bottom of the ocean. Panicked thoughts of Alex being trapped inside the fuselage flooded his mind. Desperate to fill his lungs with air he hastily lifted his head out of the water to draw another supply of oxygen into his lungs and then dived toward the sinking helicopter. In the distance he caught sight of what appeared to be Alex's long brown hair wafting in the weightless grasp of the ocean currents and didn't hesitate to swim towards it. He needed to stop for air but forced his body to deny the urgent need in fear of losing sight of her altogether. Sam's eyes remained fixed on Alex's weightless body as she sank deeper below the ocean surface. When only a short distance away he reached forward and felt his fingers trace the edges of her shoulder. He had no oxygen reserves left in his lungs but he was too close to Alex now to succumb to his body's needs. His feet thrust against the water and it felt as if an invisible hand had pushed him forward when his body propelled through the water until his hand finally closed firmly around her wrist.

With his iron-willed sights focused on the light that cut through the ocean above, he kicked with all his might until his body torpedoed through the uppermost layer of the sea as he dragged Alex to safety behind him. Exhausted by his efforts he gasped for air. It took every ounce of energy to keep both their bodies above the water level.

"Breathe, love, please!"

But Alex wasn't breathing. Sam felt his body failing under the strain of having to keep them both afloat and, with his arm firmly around her torso, swam towards a bright yellow piece of the aircraft that floated nearby. Upon reaching it he threw his free arm around it, relieved to see it was some sort of floating device attached to one of the landing skids. It took every ounce of strength in his body to hoist Alex's lifeless body up onto the floatation object. Out of breath, quelling the urge to break into tears, Sam secured his wife's body to the device and felt for a pulse. Desperate for a sign that she was still alive his fingers searched, first her wrist and then her neck, but couldn't find any sign of life. Instinctively he took a deep breath before he closed his mouth over hers and expelled air into her lungs.

"Come on, Alex. Don't do this to me! Breathe!" he said, before he drew in another breath.

But Alex didn't respond.

Sam's heart was heavy with fear. In the back of his mind he reminded himself that he was trained to remain calm in these situations and that he had done it many times before. But no matter how much he tried to let his medical experience take the lead, he knew this patient was different.

"Alex, baby, please, just breathe," he pleaded out loud.

Her face remained motionless as her body showed no response. Sam could no longer think clearly while his mouth continued to close over hers in a desperate attempt to resuscitate his wife. With his emotions now a solid lump deep in his throat, he relentlessly continued to pump mouthfuls of oxygen into her lungs.

Alex is dead, she's gone, give it up, the hollow words echoed through his mind.

"No!" he shouted out into the horizon across the dark blue ocean. Refusing to give up, he blasted another mouthful of oxygen into her mouth but nothing changed.

You need to pump her heart, his uni professor's voice rang in his head. Instantly his mind responded and his hands searched for the target spot on her torso that had already slipped off the float to where it was now halfway submerged in the water. Unable to administer the much-needed chest compressions under water he pulled her body further up out of the water and onto the helicopter's skid.

It's too late, she's gone, the dooming words sounded in his head.

"No, she's not!" he shouted and slammed his fist hard down into the hollow below her heart before he forced another mouthful of oxygen into her mouth. Alex's torso suddenly jolted as her body fought back from her demise. Moments later her lungs expelled volumes of water through her pale lips into Sam's face.

Drenched in emotion Sam watched as Alex drew in a deep breath.

"That's it, honey, breathe. I got you, just breathe." Sam's voice trembled with relief.

Overcome by emotion, Sam drew in a sharp breath as he allowed the tears to wash the salty water from his stinging eyes. As the adrenaline slowly left his body and took with it the last of his energy, his body relaxed into the water and he dropped his head onto Alex's shoulder. Aware of her small hand that gently stroked the back of his head, Sam hooked one arm over the landing skid and allowed his body to rest.

I t had been almost an hour since the crash.

"Sam," Alex whispered.

Sam groaned.

"Sam, we need to find our way out of here," her voiced croaked as a result of having taken in too much seawater. The hot sun poured down onto her face and stopped her from opening her eyes in the harsh sunlight. She squinted against it to look at Sam where his head still lay against her shoulder. He slowly lifted his head when she nudged her shoulder in an effort to wake him up. From his armpits down, his body floated in the water, held only in place by a red strap attached to the flotation device directly above

Alex's head that he had wound around one of his hands. Alex lay on her back, her upper body midway across the float, and her one leg twisted around the thin skid while the other dangled in the water.

"Are you okay?" he asked.

"I'm fine, you?"

"I'll live."

"You have a cut on your hand," Alex observed, as she raised her chin onto her chest to get a better look at the hand that he had draped over her tummy to hold her body in place.

"It's nothing," Sam said while he glanced across the ocean around them.

"It's not nothing. It looks deep."

"I'm more concerned about sharks," Sam confessed.

Instantly alert, Alex slowly shifted her bodyweight, careful not to fall off the skid. She stared across the glistening water.

"So far so good. Just don't let your hand slip into the water," she cautioned him.

"That might be difficult. There's another one of these floats over there." Sam pushed his chin towards the yellow piece of debris that drifted nearby. I'd thought of swimming over to get it."

"I'll get it," Alex said, allowing her body to slip off into the water.

She couldn't allow her mind to entertain the thought of sharks lurking below them and instead fixed her eyes on the bright yellow float as she swam closer. Similar to the device that had helped save her life, this one was also attached to a landing skid.

"Perhaps we can tie them together," she suggested when she got back to Sam.

Sam didn't answer her. Instead he stared into Alex's eyes.

"Sam, did you hear me?"

"I thought you were dead." His voice sounded low and despairing.

"I know, but I didn't die. I'm right here," Alex answered. "You saved me, Sam. You brought me back to life."

Sam dwelled on the prospect of losing her.

"I don't know what I would have done if you... without you," he caught himself.

"I'm not going anywhere, I promise. You're stuck with me," Alex smiled, "but if we don't find our way back to dry land very soon we'll both die from either hypothermia or becoming a great white's dinner. And in the event it wasn't clear before, I'm not quite ready to die yet."

"Always the fighter," Sam giggled. "Let's get on with it then."

With the two skid floats adjacent to each other, Alex and Sam managed to attach them together using the dangling straps that ran out from the rear ends. Resembling some kind of a small raft they each used remnants of the aircraft's tail as oars, and although their bodies weren't fully out of the water, the buoyant objects were at least wide enough to hold most of their weight above sea level. In the far distance, as the sunlight bounced off the ripples, they spotted the welcoming silhouette of land.

"It's most likely Cyprus," Sam guessed, feeling a bit more upbeat.

"Then I reckon we start paddling. This is the last place I want to spend the night."

But as the sun beat down on them and their exhausted bodies could no longer keep up with the demands of their dire situation, the pair soon tired. Several hours in, as the sun sank lower toward the horizon, they allowed themselves a moment to take a break and rest their arms. Pushed beyond their limits, Alex and Sam fell asleep, and as their makeshift raft hovered in the middle of the ocean, night fell around them.

CHAPTER 18

Countless hours had passed as they fought a hopeless battle against the strong ever-changing tides to reach land. Each time they tired, the strong currents sent them off course but, as exhausted and dehydrated as they were, they somehow managed to remain strapped to the helicopter's floating skids. Sam was the first to wake up as a hard object poked at his upper arm. Convinced it was nothing more than his mind that played tricks on him, he ignored it. When it happened a second time he forced his heavy eyelids open and did his best to raise his head. He couldn't and it flopped back down. As he attempted to drag himself out of his semi-conscious state he heard the faint rumblings of male voices talking among themselves in the distance. *It's a dream,* his mind told him when the drumming sound of water lapping against their makeshift raft still hushed in his ears. On his left, Alex's hand was still clasped in his. He dropped his injured hand, that had been held in place against his chest by his belt into the water to feel where the prodding came from. Another jab in the arm had him open his eyes again in sudden fear of it being a shark. The adrenaline that followed the frightening notion gave him the energy he needed so he could lift his head to have a better look. Around him it was dark for the most part, except for the bright searchlight that brought about a dark shadow that now hovered over his face. Soon after, he felt their raft being dragged across the water before hands wedged under his armpits and he was lifted onto a boat.

"Alex," he mumbled as if in a drunken stupor.

She didn't answer. He tried to look back to find her but couldn't. The voices grew louder around him and he became conscious of the sudden pain that shot up his arm before something was wrapped around his hand. Then everything went black around him.

W hen Sam came to, he found himself attached to a drip feed in a hospital.

"Alex," he called out in muted tones, eager to hear her voice.

"Shh, I'm here, Sam. You're okay. We're okay. We're in a hospital in Cyprus."

"How did we get here?"

"Some local fishermen found us. They saw the helicopter go down and set out to find us. You needed quite a few stitches in your hand and you lost a lot of blood. That's why you passed out. The doctor reckons one of the rotors might have slashed your hand during the accident."

"I guess the Greek sharks are vegetarian then," Sam chuckled.

"I guess," she smiled. "Matt's on his way. I had the hotel receptionist deliver a note. As it turns out you managed to send the pilot's video off to him moments before we crashed. That was smart." Alex was filled with pride.

"What can I say? You married well," Sam joked, before turning serious. "How many lives do you think we have left?" he asked.

Alex didn't answer. She knew where his mind was.

"Let's not worry about that right now. What's important is that we survived the crash and got back to land safely. What we do need to worry about though is freeing the pilot's family and figuring out who wants us dead and why," she said.

"Have they responded to our Facebook trap?"

"Not yet, but Red is already analyzing the video and email address you sent them. Hopefully, Matt will have answers by the time he gets here."

"Well, my logic tells me we were bugged. How else did they know to intercept our helicopter ride?" Sam said while checking the status of the I.V.

Alex stared at him as she digested his words that suddenly resonated with her and it dawned on her that Sam's theory was spot on.

"We have to let Matt know right away. I'll be back."

"You can't phone him, Alex. They might very well have his phone bugged too for all we know," Sam said, stopping her.

Alex started pacing the room as her mind attempted to come up with a solution. She knew Sam was right. If the hotel room was bugged, chances were their phones were too.

"You said Matt's on his way right, so let's just wait until he gets here. We're in a hospital, Alex. We should be safe until he gets here. We'll sweep the room and all the phones as soon as we get back," Sam assured her.

Alex remained on guard at Sam's bedside while his meds ran their course and by that evening Matt had safely sneaked Alex and Sam back into their hotel headquarters in Jerusalem. They already shared their suspicions with him and it hadn't taken long for Red to find three hidden listening devices scattered throughout the hotel suite.

"Ravid must have somehow planted them here. Snake," Matt raged.

"We've been here all along, boss. I'm fairly sure he did it using the hotel's room service," Red added.

"No wonder he hasn't fallen into our trap," Ronita added as she placed cups of tea before Alex and Sam.

"All this time he has been two steps ahead of us. It certainly explains why he's suddenly also not breathing down our necks," Matt said, more annoyed now than ever.

"Don't be so hard on yourself, Matt. At least our phones were secure so he's unaware of the fact that we know of the pilot's blackmail. We're ahead of him now," Sam said.

"And he also doesn't know the pilot's dead and that we're still alive." Alex's statement forced all eyes on her.

"You're a genius, Alex!" Matt said suddenly with newfound enthusiasm as his mind worked through her suggestion.

"Red, can you create a fake video of Alex and Sam being kicked out of the helicopter? If they get the proof they asked for they'll let the pilot's family go and if this video and email address are all we have to go on for now, we're going to use it to our advantage," Matt continued.

"You bet, boss. I'll have one done in no time," Red said as his fingers worked his keyboard.

"We need to get back to Crete." Alex jumped up as if ready to walk out the door.

"You're insane! Both of you almost got killed trying to get there, Alex," Matt protested.

"Exactly my point, Matt. Why was that, huh? What are they hiding in Crete? What don't they want us to find?" Alex argued.

"We know Ravid is The Watchman and we know we're in the middle of an illegal trade operation. It's obvious they're after Luke's ring, which we still have, might I remind you. What more do we need to know?" Matt challenged her.

"Matt, she has a point. They're hiding something. Something significant enough that you needed both rings to find it. Why would there be a hidden map if it had no meaning?" Sam questioned.

Matt paced the floor as he wrestled with their plan.

"It's too risky," he finally said. "You're safest here until we get more intel on who's behind your attempted murder. Not to mention the pilot's wife and kids are still being held ransom. I'm a government agent and I can't just ignore that."

"We're not asking you to ignore that, Matt. While you're here baiting them with the video we can be out in Crete trying to find what they don't want us to know. Besides, they'll soon believe the pilot followed through. As far as they'd be concerned we're dead," Sam said.

With his hands on his hips Matt stared at his feet in silent contemplation. He couldn't argue with that.

"Fine, but this time I'll take you. There's a small private airport south from here. I'll fly you out myself. Make sure you're armed... and I want Red to fit trackers on you. I'm not giving Ravid half a chance to slither his way back in. We're going to keep this tight. No more loose ends. Got it?"

"Agreed," Alex and Sam said simultaneously.

Matt turned to face Red.

"Where are we with that video, Red? I want it sent before we leave."

"Almost there... two more seconds... done!" Red said as he flashed the forged video on the big screen.

As they all watched a very realistic clip of Alex and Sam being pushed from the helicopter and crashing into the water, complete with their bodies floating afterwards, Red spoke. "I'm able to bypass the pilot's outgoing server and I've embedded a pixel in the footage. Once they open the video I'll be able to access the back door."

"English, boy," Matt instructed.

"The pixel is like a small ink dot with a microchip in it. It's invisible to the naked eye and collects data the moment the video is opened. With that data I then have access to their network via the IP address used to open the video. Once I'm in, I can access their server."

"I just want their location, Red," Matt said, slightly annoyed at the tech language he still didn't quite understand.

"Oh, that goes without saying. We'll have it the instant they click on it."

"Then why the complicated explanation?" Matt frowned.

"Because that's only one gold ingot. I'm taking us into the vault!" Red said with a feeling of deep satisfaction.

"We're not robbing a bank here, Red," Ronita spat.

"But we are, dear ignorant Ronnie. Forget the location, we'll have access to everything and anything on their entire server," Red bit back.

"We're not Cybercrime, Red. We're going to need a bit more detail to understand what you're on about now," Matt begged.

Red took a deep breath.

"Guys like these no doubt have a private server which they think is secure. Every single person who has ever communicated with them via text, encrypted message or email will have been banked in that server. Think of me as an invisible spider crawling through it. I'll be able to log every known and unknown associate that has ever dealt with them by accessing their server and they'll never know it. You want names? No problem. Transactions? Also not a problem. You name it and I'll have it for you before you can say trafficking takedown'."

Matt threw his arms in the air, stupefied by Red's lesson in cybercrime.

"The world has become far too complicated for me. Great work, Red. Send it off and keep me posted. I should be back in about three hours. And can we please lay off the room service?"

CHAPTER 19

As agreed, Matt flew Alex and Sam across to Crete and dropped them in a small rural field just outside Knossos. At Matt's insistence they were both armed and fitted with small satellite-tracking devices.

"Any idea where we should start?" Sam asked while the pair walked along the main road that connected the Crete capital city Heraklion with Knossos.

"Ronita sent me the coordinates to where they found the first ring. We'll start there. According to the map, it's only a short walk from here on the other side of that hill."

Alex paused as a message buzzed on her mobile phone.

"I knew it," she said.

"What?"

"The results of the bones in the ossuary came back. It's eighty percent conclusive to have belonged to Caiaphas. Their tests confirmed the bones were that of a sixty-year-old male dating back to circa AD 60."

"To think we can't even take the credit for making the discovery," Sam said.

"We can't win them all, Sam. It's a significant archaeological breakthrough in biblical history and it confirms without any uncertainty that Caiaphas wasn't just a fable. And if ever there was concrete scientific evidence proving the New Testament and the crucifixion, this would certainly facilitate the world's understanding thereof."

"See, this is why I left medicine. Nothing quite as exhilarating as proving ancient history."

Alex smiled at their mutual love for archaeology and historical discoveries.

"There it is," she announced as she spotted their destination point.

While they stood at the top of the hill, the pair stared down onto a bare triangular patch of soil that was surrounded by fruit and olive trees on two sides, and a vineyard on the third.

"Why are we looking at a production farm?" Sam asked.

"We're not looking at the fruit. We're interested in that triangular patch in the middle."

Eager to get a better look, Alex sped down the small hill and stopped in the center of the uncultivated piece of land. Her eyes skimmed over the loose rocks and sparse sprouts of grass and weeds.

"There's nothing here, Alex," Sam said while he watched Alex unfold a printed copy of a sketch.

She ignored him and turned in line with the directions marked on the sketch. A brief instant later she walked to where a small knoll protruded on the outer edge of the allotment.

"This is where they found the ring?" Sam queried while he scratched his head in confusion.

"Apparently. Except we now know the theory doesn't hold up. Caiaphas couldn't have been buried here if his bones were found in Jerusalem. This must be something else."

Alex knelt down to unpack several small archaeological tools from her backpack.

"It's worth a shot right? There's got to be something here," Alex said while she eagerly scooped at the earth with her small trowel.

"Well let's hope it's not one of the farmer's dead relatives. I can cope with it being his children's prized pet, but not his grandmother," Sam moaned.

"And you're the doctor?" Alex mocked.

"I heal people. I don't go digging up dead people."

"Now you're sounding just like Matt," she laughed,

"Can you blame me? After the other night's ordeal I reckon I'd like to stay clear from graveyards for a while."

"Well I think we'll be okay. This doesn't strike me as a graveyard. I don't see a headstone or marking of any kind here," Alex assured him as they continued to lift away the soil.

W hen an hour or so had passed, Alex finally gave up.

"I was so certain we'd find something here, Sam. I can't shake the sense that we're overlooking something. This is too obvious. If the Syrians know we have the ring, why aren't they after it? Why haven't they tried to steal it from us?"

"I haven't been able to shake that question either. Perhaps there's no bounty on it. Red didn't find any images posted online so it's possible it isn't of any value to them."

"Then why kill Nathan for it in the first place? Why did Luke run away with it only to be killed for it too?"

"But they didn't kill him for the ring. Ravid already knew we had the ring. They killed him to keep him quiet."

Alex and Sam stared at the small piles of soil around them.

"They'd already seen it, Sam! They must have. I think Nathan must have told someone about it when they first found it, without sharing his actions with his friend. That's why no one's bothered coming after the ring. They've already seen whatever they were looking to find. It all makes sense why they've been one step ahead of us all this time," Alex exclaimed, now standing next to the partially exposed mound.

"Which means they could already be here, in Knossos," Sam said, looking concerned.

"And if that's true then it means the rings do indeed hold a secret clue of some sort that could very well lead to something of far greater value. Something we need to find before they do."

Alex took the ring from her pocket and studied the symbols again closely.

"It's safe to assume they found their way here the same way we did, using both rings. Which means they must have the first ring," Alex mused out loud.

"And we have the second which we're assuming they've already seen. What if they have a replica of the second ring the same way we have a replica of the first one?"

"It's possible but highly unlikely. It took quite a lot of skill and time for Lars to recreate and he does this type of thing in his sleep. As far as we know Nathan and Luke held onto the ring from the moment they found it," Alex reasoned as she rolled Luke's ring between her fingers.

She traced the tips of her fingers over each of the three images inside the edges of the round seal. Equally spaced apart they were circled by a cable-like pattern that ran along the outer edges of the seal. None of the imprints seemed out of place in comparison to the original symbols Lars had shown her. Her eyes settled on the small raised bumps in the center between the triangularly placed symbols.

"What do you make of this?" Alex handed the ring to Sam.

"These embossed dots? It almost looks like braille, which we know is entirely impossible since it didn't even exist back then," he said.

"I don't recognize it to be any of the constellations or even planets so it must represent something on the ground."

Alex turned the ring inspecting it from all angles.

"Wait, don't you find it odd that we're standing in a triangular field that looks bizarrely close to the triangle between these three symbols on the ring? Look."

She pointed to the ring's triangular sides that perfectly matched those of the plot.

Sam leaned in over her shoulder for a better look.

"You're right. It's pretty much identical," Sam confirmed.

"Are you thinking what I'm thinking then?" Alex whispered with excitement in her eyes.

"There's only one way to find out."

With their hearts pounding excitedly against their chests, they set off to where the clusters on the ring corresponded to a position on the land.

"Do you see anything?" Sam asked

"No, but we have to assume that there would be centuries of dirt layered over whatever this cluster is. Also, if you look carefully and scale the cluster from the ring against this area, it seems each point could be rather large and proportionately spaced. I suggest we space out accordingly and start digging directly beneath each point."

Agreeing to the plan, they each claimed their spot and started digging. It took hardly any time before a dull sound escaped from beneath Sam's shovel that made them both stop.

"I heard that too. Keep going," Alex said as she waited for Sam to stab at his spot in the ground again.

Another dull thud followed that had Alex fall to her knees to scoop away handfuls of dirt on either side of Sam's spade. Sam dropped his spade and joined in.

"I've missed this," Alex said with a large grin on her face, unable to hide her excitement.

"I know. It's been a while. We could always take up gardening?" he said playfully as his big hands scooped away a substantial amount of soil.

"There!" Alex yelled when she spotted the bright blue object.

"At least we know it's not a dead body," Sam responded and slowly scooped another handful of dirt away.

Gradually the soil gave way to several more bright blue tiles that eventually met up with a single row of red tiles. Each of the blue square tiles measured exactly three inches and was placed in a perfectly spaced spiraled pattern. On the outer edges the equally sized red tiles formed a ring around the blue tiles. There, underneath the dirt, Alex and Sam unearthed a blue and red tiled column roughly one foot in diameter that stretched about three feet deep to where it joined a concrete foundation. Over the next quarter of an hour they unearthed six more columns that, when grouped together, replicated the identical cluster featured in the ring's seal.

Stunned, the pair stood back to inspect the cluster of red and blue columns in the farmland.

"Okay, that wasn't what I expected to find here at all," Sam said wryly. "Any guesses what we're looking at?"

An equally stunned Alex stared at the group of columns.

"I can only think of one thing that would resemble this and right now I'm finding it very hard for my brain to bring logic and Greek mythology together."

CHAPTER 20

"You can't be serious," Sam commented, taken aback by her observation."

"I know, I know. It sounds ridiculous to hear myself even speak it out loud, but it's the only explanation I can come up with. We're on an island in Greece, a country whose very civilization is founded and rooted in mythology."

"You're serious?"

"Sam, think about it. We've just discovered a bunch of ancient columns, which we would've never found had it not been for this ring. A ring that most likely belonged to a high priest who was alive during the first century. The Romans were very much associated with the Greeks back then so why would it not make sense to explore the idea that we've found, what I believe, to be part of the palace of King Minos?"

"Alex, are you hearing yourself? That's ridiculous. There's nothing here that says these are the ruins of a legendary ancient Minoan civilization. Are you telling me then you also believe a half-man, half-bull creature lurked among these ruins?"

"I didn't say that. All I'm saying is that these columns look identical to what historians have described the Minoan palace to be, and if I'm right, there should be a labyrinth beneath us."

Sam took two bottles of water from his bag and handed her one before he downed his.

"Look, it can't hurt to see if we can find it," Alex said when Sam fell silent. "If I'm wrong I'll be the first to admit it. But my logic tells me that if an ancient Jewish priest went to so much trouble to hide a map in his personal jewelry that led to this exact location, then it's not so farfetched to think that an underground labyrinth guarded by a legendary Minotaur would be the perfect place to hide something of great value. And while we might know better than to believe in ancient Greek myths today, back then, it was very real to the Minoan culture. Caiaphas might have only passed through here centuries after them, but that doesn't mean mythology stopped existing."

Sam's lips curled upward at the corners before he threw his hands in the air.

"Okay, you win. Even though you sound like an absolute nutcase, I've been married to you long enough to know there's not a snowball's chance in a heatwave I'd convince you otherwise." Sam placed a kiss between her brows. "So now what?"

Alex fixed her eyes on the column cluster that stretched out before them.

"Now we find a way in," she said, and started pacing between the stone structures.

"I don't see anything. Not a door or a hatch of any kind," Sam said after they'd been at it a while. "Any chance you might have been wrong about this whole labyrinth thing?" Sam asked.

Alex turned and frowned at him.

"I'm not wrong, I know it. The entrance is here somewhere. We just haven't figured it out yet."

"We've been at it all day, Alex. I'm tired," Sam complained, and sat down on one of the columns.

As soon as his buttocks hit the blue tiled surface Sam leaped off the column as a light tremor vibrated through the ground beneath it and the column slowly dropped into the limestone foundation.

"What on earth?" Sam exclaimed in shock. "Tell me I'm dreaming."

Alex shrieked with enjoyment.

"What did I tell you, huh? I knew it!" she yelled while immediately taking a seat on one of the other columns.

But when nothing happened she rose to her feet and sat down on it again. Still nothing happened.

"Maybe I'm too light. You try it," she instructed Sam.

But when Sam's second attempt was also fruitless, the pair's earlier excitement all but dissipated into the cool evening air.

"I don't understand. We did exactly as you had done with that one. Why isn't it working with the rest?" Alex said in frustration.

"Maybe there's a sequence to it, like playing a specific note at a specific time in music," Sam suggested.

"Are you hearing *yourself* now? You're suggesting musical chairs," Alex laughed.

"Hey, if you can explore the idea of an ancient man-beast living in a secret underground labyrinth then I can suggest something equally laughable."

"Okay, in all seriousness, I never said I believed in that part of the lore. But, since you met me halfway before, I'm prepared to give you the benefit of the doubt too," she said and moved to the next column.

Again, nothing happened when she sat down so they took turns and worked their way through the remaining stone structures.

"Nothing," Alex said with a heavy tone of defeat.

"There are seven columns, one of which we've managed to unlock. What if we played along with my theory of it being music notes, as idiotic as it sounds, and assume there's one of those double notes hidden in the columns?" Sam speculated.

"You mean we need to sit on two of them simultaneously."

"Exactly."

"It's worth a shot, I suppose. There's only a handful of variants it can be so let's give it a go," Alex agreed, and the duo commenced a trial and error musical chairs sequence in which they hopped between the remaining six columns.

It didn't take them long and, as with the first one, a light tremor soon vibrated between their feet when they successfully unlocked two columns on opposite ends of the cluster.

"Right then, that leaves four. So we'll just figure out the rest of the tune and we'll have your maze unlocked in no time," Sam laughed.

When they were left with one last ancient stone pillar, Alex and Sam paused in front of it.

"What if we fall through the ground?" Alex said, suddenly feeling apprehensive.

"Then you catch me," Sam joked.

But when Alex's stern face told him she didn't find him amusing, he took her hand in his and said, "We've come this far and even though I thought you were absolutely bonkers earlier, I think, your instincts were spot on. We've just uncovered an ancient combination lock, Alex, and as with all security vaults, I believe it will open a door of some kind. I seriously doubt we'll fall down a well or that we'll encounter a mythical man-beast lurking in its shadowy passages, so let's do this."

Sam's words, as always, brought Alex the assurance she needed and a slight nod had Sam turn around to take a seat on the last stone column in the cluster.

Again the ground shuddered beneath their feet and a slow grinding noise about ten feet away, caught their attention.

"There!" Sam pointed out.

The pair found themselves paused in astonishment next to a three-by-three square foot hole in the soil as they peered down onto a stone staircase that ran deep below the ground.

"Legend goes that no one ever left the labyrinth alive and if this is, in fact, the entrance to the secret labyrinth, we're as good as dead," Sam said in a low tone. "Are you sure you want to risk it?"

"No, but there's no turning back now. If it is just an ancient legendary tale then we have nothing to worry about, right?" Alex answered bravely.

With both their flashlights beaming down into the underground pit, Alex and Sam descended the eighteen stone steps into the darkness. Again a grinding noise sounded above their heads as the ancient stone slab slowly slid back into place and they were suddenly cast into pitch-black darkness.

"You were saying?" Sam whispered, now feeling even more on edge.

Apart from a rich earthy odor it was surprisingly warm as they slowly made their way along the deathly silent underground tunnel. Similar to the entrance, the tunnel was perfectly square and quite spacious, even for Sam at over six foot tall. Beneath their shoes, settled soil crunched on the untarnished limestone floor. Neither said a word while they continued to where the tunnel suddenly divided into three equally sized tunnels in front of them.

"And so we have our labyrinth it seems," Sam said wryly.

"We're not splitting up so pick one," Alex whispered, conscious that their voices carried through the hollow underground passages.

"Left, right or straight ahead," Sam contemplated their options out loud.

"Wait! What's this?" Alex stopped and whispered as she pointed to a small, barely noticeable etching in the stone directly above the left passage.

"It almost looks like... no, that can't be, can it?" Sam whispered as his mind tried to make sense of the outlines of a cross.

"It is! It's a Knights Templar cross. I'm sure of it," Alex said overflowing with excitement.

"This must be it then. It's a well-known fact that they used secret underground passages all over the world to move around. I just wouldn't have ever guessed Crete was on that list, but I say we take the left tunnel," Sam said with conviction.

With newfound confidence, they followed the tunnel which turned and changed direction a few times, and they soon found themselves having to face another crossroads. This time, however, there were only two tunnels to choose from.

"Left or right?" Sam asked, while his eyes searched the walls for another cross and found none.

"It looks as if we're on our own with this one. There's no markings of any kind anywhere," Alex answered as her hands continued to glide over the surfaces of the walls.

"I say we stick with left," Sam suggested.

"What if that's the obvious choice and it's a trap?"

"You mean there might be a Minotaur waiting for us at the other end," Sam joked.

"Actually, I meant it's a dead end or a booby trap or something."

"Then let's take the one on the right," Sam said casually as he turned towards it.

"No, you're correct. Let's stick with the left," Alex stopped him.

"Is that your final answer or do you want to call a friend?" he said playfully.

"Oh, that's funny." Alex smiled with a fake smile while she shone the torch below her chin. "I just think it's safer to assume the cross was a general instruction to steer left with all the tunnels," she then added.

"Left it is then, wifey. After you."

CHAPTER 21

As it turned out the left tunnel hit a dead end very soon and Alex and Sam found themselves having to turn back.

"So the obvious didn't pan out. I reckon we throw logic out the window," Alex said, leaving Sam to suppress a smile.

Having reached the intersection, they turned into the second tunnel, which also hit a dead end.

"I don't understand. Did we miss a junction?" Alex said puzzled as she stood staring at the closed off wall in front of them.

"Not unless I fell asleep somewhere along the line, no."

"Well then, how could both lead to a dead end? Unless—"

"We were supposed to take one of the other two tunnels at the first intersection," Sam finished her thought.

"We took the left one because of the cross above it but there were two other passages. The Templars must have done that intentionally. That's why neither of these two passages had a cross. We need to go back." Alex turned and set off at a quick pace back to the first junction with Sam close on her heels.

"Right or straight ahead?" Sam posed the question once they reached the first two tunnels again.

"Let's head straight. If it turns into a dead end then we just turn back again, right?" Alex answered.

But as they set off down the tunnel they soon realized there was no end in sight. It seemed to stretch on forever, turning left and right several times. And as with all mazes, the tunnel eventually exited into a large circular chamber from which a dozen more dark passages beckoned.

"Well, I guess that was inevitable. What's better than to be trapped in a menacing network of dark underground passages? Now I know why no one survived. This could take an eternity," Sam said sarcastically.

Alex ignored him and walked into the center of the underground cavern. Under the beam of her flashlight, she searched for a way forward but each tunnel looked identical. Human remains lay scattered across sections of the floor and suddenly it felt eerie and foreboding

"There's no way we're going to find our way out of here is there?" Sam said.

"There's always a way. We just have to keep our heads and not let our emotions get the better of us."

"She says with a dozen skeletons lying around. I don't like this, Alex. Something feels off."

Alex felt it too. Almost as if something horrible was about to happen.

"Okay, let's stay calm and focus on what we came here for," Sam said, trying to regain control of his flailing emotions. "The ring brought us here. There has to be something we're meant to find. We just need to look for clues," he continued, and joined Alex where she was now shining her torch onto a pile of bones that lay close to one of the tunnels.

"It's not human," Sam remarked as he knelt down beside it.

"Then what is it?"

"Not sure. I've never seen anything like it."

Alex moved closer to the tunnel and shone her flashlight inside.

"This one's a dead end but I think I have an idea," she said as she pulled her mobile phone from her pocket.

"I don't think you'll get any signal down here, Alex."

"No need. Red insisted on installing this sonar app on my phone. It doesn't require the phone to be linked to a service. This particular situation is precisely what it is designed for and I think it can help us find our way out of here. When submarines are under water they use active sonar to find their way. They emit pulses of sound waves that travel through the water and when they hit their target, it reflects back. Bats, dolphins and whales use the same technique to catch their prey. This app does exactly that. Once it sends out the pulses and records the returned data it builds a grid. We'll be able to see which tunnel leads out of here; at least I hope we will."

"Sounds like all they needed to survive down here was a cell phone. Remind me to thank Red when we get out of here. It wouldn't surprise me if our recent near fatal sea adventure was what prompted him to create the application. He's a clever one, I tell you. Give it a go. I'd be lying if I told you I like it down here. This place gives me the creeps," Sam said with a shiver down his spine.

Alex didn't waste any time. With the mobile application activated she quickly set about scanning each of the tunnels that led out from the chamber while Sam continued to search for clues that might help them find the ring's hidden trove.

"What was that?" A sudden noise caught Sam's attention.

"I heard it too. It sounded like a rumbling noise," Alex whispered back.

"Anytime you want to get us out of here is good," Sam hinted for Alex to hurry up.

"Almost there. I have one more tunnel left."

Another low rumbling, that sounded louder than the previous one, echoed through the chamber. The unidentified sound left them both on edge.

"What is that?" Alex asked as her trembling fingers violently tapped her mobile's screen.

"I don't know, but I do know I don't want to wait around to find out. Please tell me your fancy app worked" Sam begged, while he nervously moved the light from his torch between the tunnels in anticipation that something evil might surprise them at any moment.

"This way!" Alex said when a bright green labyrinth grid finally flashed across her phone's screen.

The rumblings grew louder and more frequent as they ran towards the tunnel that, according to the accumulated sonar data, showed their way out.

They didn't dare to look back at whatever had caused the guttural sounds that had all the hairs on their necks stand up with fear, nor did they try to speak to each other. They just ran, as fast as their feet could carry them. Until they reached the end of the tunnel and they were forced to stop.

CHAPTER 22

Greeted by a solid wall it felt as if they'd been punched in the stomach. Alex stared at the grid on her phone. They stood exactly where the app showed the exit was supposed to be.

"Well, there goes that gadget," Sam said as he tried to catch his breath while he shone his flashlight back down the passage.

"This is the exit, Sam. It has to be." Alex turned her phone off and popped it back into her pocket. Her hands glided across the wall in search of anything that might indicate an exit point. Behind them the rumbling sound changed and suddenly it became frightfully familiar as it grew louder and louder by the second.

"It's water!" They said in unison.

Not wasting any time Sam turned around and shone his torch onto the walls and then onto the floor beneath their feet. "Forget the sonar. We're going to need a submarine if we don't get out of here very soon! This place is about to be flooded!"

The rushing sound of fast-moving water grew louder and stronger and they now felt its vibrations push through the walls and the floor.

Alex shrieked, a panicked cry of desperation. "There's nothing here, Sam!"

Sam didn't answer. His eyes were fixed on the tiny Templar's cross that was carved out into a slightly raised stone in the floor near the wall. Behind them the rapidly flowing water entered their tunnel.

"Here goes nothing," Sam yelled in hope and pushed the ball of his foot down onto the Templar cross. He felt his wife's trembling hand grab onto his moments before the now familiar grinding noise of stone against stone sounded in their ears. Trapped between the painstakingly slow-moving slab and the volumes of water that rapidly pushed closer towards them a mere twenty feet behind, they squarely stared death in the face. A welcome rush of wind greeted them as the stone slowly moved away from the tunnel's wall. Not wasting a second, Sam wedged his fingers into the narrow cavity between the door and the wall. Using every ounce of strength he pushed the stone door in a desperate effort to speed it up until the space was big enough for Alex to slip through. He briefly turned his head to assess the ever-increasing flood of water that threatened to drown them any moment now.

"Go!" He shouted at Alex to squeeze through the narrow opening first.

Alex's slim body slipped through the tight space easily but Sam couldn't get more than his right leg and arm through. Desperate to free her husband, Alex yanked Sam's arm from the other side with no success. Having now run out of time a massive wave of water slammed hard against Sam's feet and all along the side of his leg.

"Go, Alex, get out of here!"

"I'm not leaving you!"

Sam's eyes traced his wife's silhouette that was only made visible in the faint moonlight that shone towards him from the other side of the stone door.

Without warning the water was upon him and Sam felt his body thrown off balance under the strong water that thrust against his shoulder and the side of his face. Ironically, the force was exactly what he needed to squeeze the last bit of his body through the narrow opening. Finally freed from the stone vice, Sam stumbled through the ever-rising, waist-deep water toward the tunnel's exit. He kept his eyes on Alex who was only a few feet in front of him, gripped by the knowledge that it was only a matter of time before the water would come flooding toward him. He also didn't dare look back when his ears told him it was already too late. The river of water burst through the half-opened stone door and shattered it to pieces before it swept their powerless bodies along with it. The tunnel belched a compressed river of water so strong that it ejected both of them through an overhead opening which had them flying through the air before it spat them out onto the ground.

Their bodies thumped down hard onto a stone floor where they lay disorientated while making every effort to rid their lungs of water. When Alex finally got her breath back she turned to inspect their surroundings. The water had spread out across the ground beneath their bodies and they were no longer in danger. It was nighttime but the full moon illuminated the area to reveal they had managed to safely make it out from beneath the ground.

"I never thought I'd be happier to see the moon than right now," she smiled.

"You can say that again. I feel as if I'd just escaped the belly of an ancient beast."

"Yeah, well, beast it certainly wasn't. At least we've now proven the Minotaur is nothing but an underground labyrinth that killed its prisoners by drowning. I'm sure fooling the people into thinking it was a fierce man-eating beast was quite the entertainment to the deceitful king back then. A fabricated myth that managed to survive centuries."

Sam straightened up before he helped Alex to her feet.

"What is this place?" she remarked as she stood staring at a mural of blue and white painted dolphins above her head.

"Oh, you ain't seen nothing yet, wifey. Look what the beast spat out." Sam's excited voice caused her to turn around.

Sam stood next to a heap of broken clay vessels. Almost in disbelief, his eyes fixed on one particular spot where he had focused his flashlight. Lying upside down beneath the scattered pieces of pottery lay a rectangular iron box roughly the size of a jewelry box. Alex bent down to pick it up.

"It's actually really heavy," she commented with surprise and placed it down on top of a disintegrated stone wall next to them.

"What do you think it is?"

"I'm not sure. It's definitely made from an iron-like metal and judging from the unequal patterns I'd guess it was hand carved. I can tell you for sure that it's not Minoan."

"How do you know?"

"It has an image of Christ on the left and one of Mary on the opposite end on the back panel. Then this here is Hebrew writing." Alex pointed to the top of the box.

"And I'm guessing you have no idea what it says."

Alex reached for the translation app on her phone.

"My phone didn't survive the water. How about yours?"

Sam pulled his mobile from his pocket.

"I'm afraid it's busted too."

Alex turned her attention back to the box and inspected it more closely from the front.

"It's locked. There's some kind of weird latch."

"That's definitely an original. I've never seen anything like it in this century."

Alex turned her attention to the area around them. Her eyes skimmed over the very uneven stone floor beneath their feet. Somewhat symmetrically shaped stone slabs were joined in no particular pattern to form a large surface surrounded by badly deteriorated walls that were missing in several places. Three pillars painted a deep red hue stood on their own to one side and behind them were the remnants of a small room that might have once been attached to the pillars. One of the walls was painted with a large colorful scene of a half-man, half-bull attacking a Minoan. The image stretched all the way across the roughly six-foot-high by eight-foot-wide wall. In the middle of the room was a large stone basin that almost looked like a modern firepit. Apart from that there was nothing but two clay pots in the farthest corner.

"There's something inside," Sam said when he shook the box and instantly drew Alex's attention back to their fortunate find.

"I'll bet you a romantic home-cooked dinner this is exactly what we were meant to somehow find," Sam said with a mischievous look on his face.

"You're saying the map in the rings led us here for this?"

"Absolutely! We just didn't have a clue where it was. I don't believe it was a coincidence either. This here looks like it could have been some queen's jewelry box and for all we know there's a dazzling gold ruby encrusted necklace in here. Maybe that's why it's so heavy."

Alex frowned at Sam's silly theory.

"That's the most ridiculous thing I've ever heard you say, Sam. I hope you're preparing yourself to lose that bet."

"I know I'm not wrong, Alex. I say we get back to HQ and break this baby open. Ancient boxes are only locked if they're hiding something of significant importance inside."

"Unless it's filled with a dead king's ashes or bones."

"Well I guess we'll see, Mrs. Quinn, and if I'm right, you're going to make me your mother's famous venison pie."

"Deal. Now, if you're done fooling around can we please get back to Jerusalem before the Syrians catch up with us?"

"Now that you mention them, don't you find it strange that they haven't found this place yet? They must have deciphered the map the same way we have."

"Perhaps they just haven't figured out the clusters and the musical chairs yet. And let's not forget that, even if they did make it underground, they'd still have to fight off the Minotaur."

The pair broke into high-spirited giggles at Alex's witticism while they transferred the heavy metal box into Sam's backpack and hastily set off toward the rural field where they'd agreed upfront that Matt would collect them at sunrise.

CHAPTER 23

The crisp four a.m. air amplified their footsteps as they strode along the cobbled pathways between the palace ruins. Situated on top of a large hill in Knossos the palace overlooked the green valley below. Alex and Sam easily determined their direction and walked north toward their agreed pick-up point. The earthy smell of a nearby olive grove wafted through the night air. Above them the sky was clear and the full moon illuminated their way for miles. Deathly quiet, apart from a nearby owl that hooted and made its nocturnal presence known, there wasn't a single soul in sight anywhere. So when a set of footsteps echoed through the stillness of the night behind them, Alex and Sam's bodies immediately tensed up.

"I heard it too," Alex whispered to Sam when she picked up on his body language next to her. Neither stopped to look behind them. Instead, they continued as if nothing was wrong. A brief moment of doubt flooded Alex's mind but when the footsteps sounded again, she knew without a shadow of a doubt they were being followed. Her mind focused on the usual spot where she kept her gun in the small of her back, sensing its familiar lines against her skin. Next to her she sensed the tension in Sam's body as his gait increased ever so slightly. Her eyes trailed to where Sam's hands pulled the straps of his backpack tighter over the front of his shoulders and then around his waist. They were about a thirty-minute walk away from the small field that lay in the middle of a local farmer's vineyards in the direction of Heraklion. Sunrise was around six a.m. so Matt wouldn't be there yet.

The cobbled pathway that led away from the palace ruins soon joined a dirt road. As their feet crunched on the loose grit they listened closely for the third set of footsteps, counting the paces to estimate the distance between them. Thirty paces into the dirt road they heard them crunch noisily behind them.

"There's more than one, Alex," Sam whispered when he distinguished at least two more sets of footsteps. Alex searched for a way out. On either side of the single-track dirt road was nothing except low thorny bushes. She recognized the thorns to be the same as the ones found along the hill where they'd first gone after Luke outside the Old City. With nowhere to go but straight ahead, Alex and Sam increased their pace. If whoever was following them wanted them dead they'd have shot them already. They were an easy target and, knowing that, it meant they must want them alive, and quite possibly knew they had found the box. As if Sam's mind was interlinked with hers, he whispered, "Do you think they were spying on us back at the ruins?"

"It certainly seems that way. They could've easily killed us already but they haven't which can only mean they know we've found the box."

"We can't lead them to the rendezvous point. It will put Matt's life in danger too."

Alex knew Sam was correct. They'd have to find another way there and lose their stalkers along the way, but running away from them would be a cowardly way out for Alex.

"How many of them do you think there are?" Alex whispered.

"I count at least three. Why, what are you thinking? Forget I asked," Sam quickly retracted his question. He'd figured it out already.

Alex slowed her pace. She was ready. Her gun was loaded and if there were only three it should be child's play.

"That's a bad idea, Alex. We don't know anything about them or what they're capable of. They'll most certainly be armed, plus I could be totally wrong and we could face far more than just three. There's no way to be sure without turning around to get a proper look and then they'll know we're on to them."

"I counted three as well. We can easily take them down, Sam. Nothing we haven't handled before. Besides, do you have a better idea?"

"Can't we just outrun them?" Sam knew he was wasting his breath but it didn't hurt to ask.

"Fine, have it your way," he conceded, "I can't say I'm not curious to find out who they are."

He slowed his pace to meet hers, unable to resist sneaking a look over his shoulder from the corner of his eye.

"Yup, we have three, about twenty yards behind us."

"And, by my calculations we're roughly fifteen minutes out from our marker. Let's veer off the road through those bushes up ahead and cross into the vineyard. They'll follow us in and then we ambush them."

Sam gave Alex a thumbs-up and followed her lead between the thorny shrubs along the shoulder of the road. As predicted, the pursuers trailed them in and it soon became a silent game of cat and mouse between the vines. When Alex and Sam reached the middle of the vineyard they split sideways in opposite directions before they quietly worked their individual ways back towards the direction of the dirt road. The plan was to surprise their stalkers from behind. It worked, and Alex and Sam soon found themselves closing in on the oblivious trio from behind. Using their combat-trained signaling only, Alex and Sam stealthily moved forward between the vines until they were a mere three feet away and all the while remained completely undetected by their hunters who had now become the prey. They'd agreed not to use their guns so as to not alert the authorities and so, in perfect tandem, without sounding as much as a twig snapping beneath their shoes, Alex and Sam leaped forward and took the three men down. A single punch in the kidneys followed by a few perfectly executed forceful martial arts kicks, had all three men's faces buried in the fertile ground between the vines in all of ten seconds. They never saw it coming. Sam flipped one of the unconscious men over and stared at his face. Frowns were exchanged between the powerful duo, after which Sam promptly turned the other two men over also.

"They're not Syrian," Alex said surprised. "I don't understand. I thought they were the guys from Jerusalem," she continued.

Stunned by their discovery Sam didn't say a word. His eyes examined the three men who were casually dressed in jeans and T-shirts. He leaned over and scooped up the dark blue baseball cap that lay upside down next to one of them and traced the oddly shaped white embroidered letter on the front.

"They're American," Sam announced.

"American? That makes no sense. What makes you say that?"

"This cap. I don't know much about American sports but if I'm not mistaken then this is a baseball cap."

"That doesn't mean they're American, Sam. You can pick these caps up from any street market anywhere in Europe. It's probably a cheap knock-off."

"Not according to the official Detroit Tigers label inside."

Sam shone his flashlight on the cap's label and extended it towards Alex.

"Why would three ordinary looking Americans be after us?" Alex murmured under her breath as she watched Sam pat them down in search of their identities. Instead he retrieved a .38 special revolver off each of them.

"Since when do ordinary men carry weapons?" Sam said as he emptied the bullets from the cylinders into his hand.

"They're not military, that's for sure, they never saw us coming nor did they have their guns drawn. Not to mention that .38 specials are ordinary defense weapons and available from just about anywhere. It's kind of the go-to gun for self-defense, isn't it? There's nothing that says professional about these three."

"I agree. They look more like amateurs who planned a local domestic robbery."

"Perhaps they don't know anything about the rings and they're just druggies who accidentally stumbled upon us and thought they'd score a quick buck."

"Maybe."

Sam glanced at his wristwatch. "We need to get moving. The sun is going to be up soon. He stowed the eighteen bullets in one of the small pockets of his backpack and ushered Alex back towards the road.

Fifteen minutes later they reached their pickup point and soon heard Matt's chopper in the far distance. It wasn't until Matt hovered just above them and they could see his worried face, that they became aware of sudden danger.

"Get in!" Matt yelled above the noise of the engine without setting the helicopter down.

A single bullet whistled past Alex's head as she reached up to take hold of the landing skid. When another few bullets fired at them in quick succession she turned and set eyes on a fast-approaching black dune buggy. She instinctively drew her gun and fired back, just missing the buggy's wheel. Next to her, Sam had reacted the same and fired two bullets toward the vehicle. Several bullets clanked off the chopper's skids and forced Matt to move from his hovering position. Alex took aim and fired a single bullet into the buggy's left wheel, causing it to lose control before it flipped over and rolled onto its side.

"Come on, come on!" Matt shouted from where he hovered behind them.

Grabbing the brief window of opportunity Alex and Sam turned to leap into the chopper. With Alex barely inside the cabin, a fresh round of gunfire descended upon them and clanked loudly against the helicopter's frame. She fired back to cover Sam but it was too late. Sam's upper body thrust forward into the helicopter cabin and onto the floor.

"Sam!" Alex yelled and dropped her gun to free up her hands.

She wrapped her fists around his backpack's shoulder straps and yanked back to pull Sam's limp body into the aircraft. At over six feet tall with the helicopter still hovering four feet above the ground, Sam's body was heavy and worked against her efforts. With her hands still gripped around the straps she fell.

"Come on, Alex, pull him in! We've got to get out of here!" Matt urged.

Alex wedged her feet against the helicopter's frame and gave two hard tugs while Matt dipped the chopper to aid the momentum. It worked and Sam's body slid forward on top of Alex inside the cabin.

CHAPTER 24

"Sam, baby, wake up!" Alex yelled but Sam didn't move.

With Sam now turned on his back beside her on the floor of the helicopter cabin, her trembling hand gently tapped against his cheek but yielded no response whatsoever.

"He's not breathing, Matt!" Alex screamed once he had managed to get the helicopter high enough into the air and out from under another onslaught of bullets.

"Where was he hit?"

"I don't know. I can't see any blood anywhere." Alex panicked as her hands and eyes scanned Sam's body. She slapped his cheeks again. A pool of tears flooded her eyes and blurred her vision. Still there was no response. She closed her lips over his mouth and expelled the air from her lungs into his. As she waited for his body to respond she silently begged the God he believed in to save him. The tears flowed freely from her eyes and she felt numb with fear of losing him.

"Keep trying, Alex. We're almost at the hospital!" Matt encouraged from the cockpit.

His words jerked Alex back into the present and she exhaled another supply of oxygen into Sam's mouth.

"Please, Sam, just breathe," she cried.

But when nothing happened, the glimmer of hope she had left quickly disappeared, and a new wave of panic pushed through the hollow cavities of her chest again. Knelt next to him she gently kissed his cheek while her tears flowed freely onto his face.

"Don't do this to me. You can't leave me now," she cried.

In another final and desperate attempt to save her husband's life, Alex wiped the tears from her face and, in a brief moment of sanity, pumped his chest with her hands before blowing another supply of oxygen into his mouth.

Sam's eyes gradually opened as his body finally responded and he drew in a sudden deep breath.

In one simultaneous motion Alex felt her tensed up muscles release all her fears while her heart shed the dead weight it had been imprisoned by. A barely audible whimper escaped from between her lips as she lowered her mouth onto his cheek.

"I thought I'd lost you."

As Sam's breathing returned to normal, he groaned in pain when he tried to sit up.

"Just take it easy, mate. We're not far from the hospital now," an equally relieved Matt assured his friend.

"It's okay, just breathe. I got you. Where are you hurt?" Alex asked, still confused about the lack of visible blood on his body.

"My back hurts and I feel like I've been sucker punched in the stomach."

"Let's get your backpack off. I can't see anything."

With Sam now in a seated position and the backpack on the seat in front of them, Alex lifted his shirt to inspect his back.

"There's nothing here. Not a single gunshot wound. Just the beginnings of a massive bruise across your lungs, but nothing else. Not even a hole in your shirt."

She raised his shirt and scanned across his abdomen and chest.

"Again, nothing. I don't understand. How were you shot and not breathing but there's no entry wound anywhere?"

"I think I know why," Sam said, coughing as his chin pushed toward his backpack on the seat in front of him.

Alex stared at the gaping bullet hole in the backpack. She pushed her index finger through the panel to where it collided with the ancient metal box inside the bag. Stunned in anticipation of the answer she already knew, she unzipped the bag to remove the box and then placed it on top of the seat. A single bullet implanted in the metal stunned the pair into silence. Its position was what had caught them by surprise. There, buried in the hands of Christ's engraved image, the stark contrasting lead tip declared more than the answer they were looking for.

"And that there, is precisely what faith is all about," Sam said as he rested his head back against the pilot's seat.

Stunned beyond words, Alex stared at the box that had miraculously saved her husband's life.

"Blimey, mate, it knocked your wind out under the impact from the bullet. I've never seen anything like it. You're one lucky man, mate. How about we get you kids back to our hotel headquarters so you can recover properly?"

"Music to my ears, mate. Nothing a hot shower and a warm bed can't fix. But if you throw in a good stew, I'll be up and at it in no time," Sam playfully responded to Matt.

The remainder of their trip was in complete silence as each of them digested the events and soon they touched down on the roof of their hotel in Jerusalem. The time in the helicopter had given

Sam the rest his body required to heal enough that, apart from being bruised and stiff, he was beginning to feel almost normal again.

"Right then, let's see what you two found back in Knossos," Matt said when they all sat at the table an hour later.

"Apart from a near fatal battle against a mythical creature who, up until now had been living in an underground labyrinth beneath the Minoan king's palace, we found this."

Alex placed the metal box in the center of the table.

"You fought a mythical creature?" Red said in surprise.

"That's what you focus on, really?" Ronita challenged.

"Battling beasts sounds far more exciting than staring at a metal shoebox," Red bit back.

"Shows you how much you know. This *shoebox* probably has a valuable ancient treasure inside, but if you'd rather focus your tiny brain on imaginary beasts, be my guest."

"Are you two adolescents done? You're worse than my two ten-year-old nephews back home."

"Sorry, boss," Ronita apologized while Red returned to his desk and hid behind his screens.

Matt turned to Alex.

"What do we know?"

"Not much, except that it's clearly not Minoan and there's something locked inside."

"And that whatever is inside is important enough to someone who almost killed you for it. You said they were American. How did we suddenly go from a Syrian trafficking syndicate to the American mob?" Matt's voice was laced with frustration.

"Beats me. Any results from the social media bait?" Sam asked.

"Nothing. Not even a nibble. Red's still working on tracking them through the video but that could take a while, if ever. Who knows what filters they've masked their server with. For all we know they're bouncing several signals off towers all across the world."

"They can't hide from me, boss. I'll find them." Red tried to redeem himself.

"We'll soon find out won't we, smarty pants. Maybe if you keep your childish squabbles out of the workplace and focus on the job at hand we'll get there faster."

"Sorry, boss."

"I'm sure they're doing the best they can, Matt. We all are. We'll figure it out soon enough," Sam said.

Matt didn't respond and the room fell quiet with tension.

"We do have this box though and while we might not quite know who's after it, perhaps it will get us closer to finding out. It has these Hebrew letters on it but I don't yet know what they mean." Alex diverted their attention to the box.

"I'm on it," Ronita jumped in, eager to reclaim her boss's favor and get their mission back on track. In less than thirty seconds, she had translated the text.

"It says, '*Yahweh*'."

"What does that mean?" Alex asked.

"According to this it's the name by which God revealed Himself to Moses when He gave him the ten commandments. It's said the name was extremely sacred and used only by the holiest of Jewish high priests during Passover."

"So this box belonged to Caiaphas also," Matt deduced.

"It certainly seems that way," Ronita confirmed.

"There's only one way of finding out for sure. Let's break this baby open," Matt said, eager to see the contents of the box and lift his team's spirits.

"Ready?"

The team nodded in agreement. It only took two knocks on the back of a screwdriver to pop the ancient lock open.

"You do the honors since you almost lost your life and all, mate," Matt said to Sam.

Sam didn't need to be invited twice and as the room waited in anticipatory silence to see a box loaded with ancient jewels, he flipped the lid open.

There, between layers of crimson cotton cloth lay an ancient scroll that instantly captured their attention.

Alex carefully lifted the five-inch scroll from the box and rolled it between her fingers until their eyes caught sight of the bright red wax seal that held the parchment in place.

"It's the seal, from the ring," she announced.

"So it's confirmed to be this Caiaphas fellow's then."

"Open it," Sam encouraged and handed Alex a surgical knife from their tool bag.

Alex inserted the steel blade between the parchment and the wax and carefully sliced it away from the fragile paper. Preserving the seal inside the box she unrolled the document and gently spread it open on the table. It was roughly eight and a half by five inches wide and contained a single passage written with red ink in what appeared to be Hebrew.

Ronita instantly turned to her computer translation program while Alex studied the document further.

"I could be wrong but I think this ink is mercury sulfide, the same ink used on the Dead Sea scrolls that were discovered in the late 1940s and early 1950s. This ink was usually reserved for important documents only. It's remarkable," Alex said.

"Well, we have ourselves a clue, or a riddle it seems," Ronita reported as she read out the translated ancient text.

Says the Lord who washes away my iniquity
The crown has fallen from my head
I bury my shame and regret between the scarlet thread
Look upon the son of David, oh, Judah
Beneath the covenant of our Lord most high
Where the father of many sons sacrificed one
And the Almighty one prophesied
With this my atonement unto Thee
In the hope to forever be set free

"Signed Josephus, son of Caiaphas," Ronita added.

CHAPTER 25

"I feel like I've just been to Sunday school. Can anyone please explain what I'm supposed to make of this?" Matt said as he fidgeted with a pen on the table. It was no secret by now that talking about Christianity made him very uncomfortable.

"You're not alone, Matt. If I hadn't seen it with my own eyes I would have sworn it was a page from the Bible," Alex confessed. "But what I do know for sure is that Ronita is right. It is a clue."

"And a confession," Sam added.

"What makes you say that?" Alex asked.

"I really have my work cut out with you lot. It's very obvious. He's using phrases implying remorse and confesses that he'd sinned. There are several scriptures all over the

235

Bible talking about repentance and atonement. These words literally mean to show regret for your sins, turning away from them and trying to correct them. Look, 'the crown has fallen from my head.' He no longer feels worthy of being called a servant of God, a high priest. He buries his shame in regret between the scarlet thread, signifying redemption that binds Genesis with Revelation, the beginning and the end, pivoting on the sacrificial death of Jesus Christ on the cross. At least that's what makes up the first three lines of the text."

"What about the rest? What do you make of that?" Matt asked.

"That's a clue without a doubt. Not impossible to figure out actually. If Caiaphas intended on hiding something he wasn't exactly a genius in that department. I would also go so far as claiming this wasn't as much about hiding something as it was about confessing his sin and seeking forgiveness for it," Sam said.

"I think you're right. The last two lines literally says he hopes it will set him free," Alex added.

"So if it's just an insignificant riddle that leads to a sacrifice of some sorts, why is someone trying so hard to get their hands on it?" Ronita asked, looking rather puzzled.

"Who knows? All I know is that we need to figure this puzzle out and fast. Someone out there knows a whole lot more than us and they clearly don't care who they hurt in the process to get their hands on the treasure."

"Uh, boss, you might want to come have a look at this," Red's nervous voice broke through the team's confusion.

Matt moved in behind Red and stared at his garbled computer screen.

"And, what are we looking at?"

Red shuffled anxiously in his chair.

"Go on then, boy. What did you dig up that's so important?"

"You're looking at an embedded ad on the Dark Web," Red answered.

"What's that?"

"Did I just hear you say the Dark Web?" Sam called out from where he now sat up in his chair.

"You know about it," Red queried.

"Who doesn't? It's only the most clandestine part of the World Wide Web. Every underground syndicate on the planet uses it to remain anonymous and carry out illegal activities that are totally unseen to the normal internet user. If you want to remain untraceable then that's the place to do your illegal business."

The entire team stared at Sam in astonishment, their eyes filled with questions as they waited for Sam to explain his knowledge.

"Okay, so I might have had a distant cousin who dabbled in all things web related, so I read up on it. No big deal. I've never accessed it. You need special software and really need to know your way around the stuff to gain access anyway. Tell them, Red." Sam winked at Red to save him from the imminent line of questions.

Red cleared his throat. "He's indeed one hundred percent correct, yes. I'd keep a close eye on him if I were you though," he said in jest.

"Okay, jokes aside. You said it was an advert. For what?" Alex brought them back to matters at hand.

"An ad to find the Caiaphas code," Red read out.

Matt let out a confused grunt and rubbed the back of his head in frustration.

"Wait, you've lost me. You mean to say someone out there, in the deep underground of the Web placed a secret advertisement in their classifieds, recruiting people to hunt down this scroll?"

Red nodded.

"Who placed the ad?"

"They don't have names in the darknet, boss. It's all encrypted with code names and usernames. That's the whole idea. It's anonymous."

"How much? What's he offering in exchange for the code?" Alex asked.

"Ten million American dollars."

Matt let out a prolonged whistle of surprise.

"That's quite the commission."

"That's just half of it, boss. If they decipher the code and find some kind of holy relic, they get an additional ten million."

"You're not serious. What can be worth that much money?" Ronita asked.

Matt paced the room while he deliberated his thoughts out loud.

"Okay, so whoever this is, is offering American dollars. You were attacked by ordinary looking Americans. The second lot in the dune buggy looked like they could have been Russian, and let's not forget our Syrian syndicate over here. Are you telling me we have all these Dark Web crazies from all over the world running about trying to find this scroll?"

"You said you wanted the head of the snake, didn't you, mate? My guess is the Syrians saw the advert and, since this is their home turf and what they do anyway, they got a head start on the rest."

"And Nathan and Luke somehow accidentally got caught up in the treasure hunt by finding the ring. Whoever Nathan showed the ring to after they'd found it, must have spread the word, and before they knew it, they were smack bang in the center of an international treasure hunt," Alex added.

Matt took his usual contemplative position at the window.

"And somehow you managed to find it first which means we're literally an open target in a massive scavenger hunt."

"Yeah, like our own *Hunger Games*," Red laughed.

"How do you find this funny? This is serious, Red," Ronita scolded.

This time it was Red's turn to ignore his snappy colleague.

"Boss, we're not using our heads. We're light years ahead of these guys. We actually *have* the code. They don't. If Alex and Sam can decipher it, find whatever's at the end of the rainbow, we simply reply to the advertisement and lead them into a trap to do the exchange. It's not rocket science."

Matt didn't answer. Instead he poured himself a fresh coffee after which he turned to face Alex.

"It's up to you, Sheila. I brought you in on this and by the looks of things, we're up against the entire world on this mission. We have no idea who the puppetmaster is and what or whom we're really facing. But, I have the full resources of every government agency in the world at my disposal and I can have a tactical team up and running here in less than eight hours. It depends whether you're up for it. It's risky as heck but it's your call."

Alex hesitated; something she'd never done before. Things were very different now and Sam had almost died. She turned to face him and saw that he recognized the doubt in her eyes.

"We've got this, Alex. Nothing we haven't done before. And this time we're not alone. We have Matt and the rest of the team. We know what we're up against and I think I've already figured out where the clue leads. Let's finish this and bring the entire lot down. Besides, instinct tells me this is about something far bigger than any of us."

Alex dropped her shoulders in despair as a jumble of fear and trepidation rushed through her body.

"I don't know about this, Sam. You were almost killed this morning. Twenty million dollars is a big paycheck and enough motivation to take someone's life over. I thought I'd lost you today. I can't—"

"You're not going to lose me. I'm fine. We'll be extra cautious and Matt's got our backs." Sam briefly paused before he turned in his seat and leaned in to speak to Alex more privately.

"I've never told you this, Alex, but as a boy growing up in a Christian home I've always felt I was called to something bigger... a higher purpose. I thought it was saving people's lives, which is why I surrendered to my father's wishes of becoming a doctor. But after years in the medical profession the feeling never went away. That's part of why I stepped away from it and joined you. I'd hoped it would clear my head or provide direction of some kind. Now, years later, we're here, in the Holy Land and somehow I feel my life's journey brought me here, today, to exactly the place I was always meant to be. And I'm literally holding a biblical artifact that belonged to the very man who condemned the God I've served all my life. I can't turn my back on this now. I have to see where it leads. That metal box miraculously saved my life and I can't ignore it."

Alex looked at her husband with stunned eyes. In all the time they'd been together she had never asked him about the times he'd 'run an errand' on a Sunday morning and the Bible that was on his nightstand. Now, it all made perfect sense.

"I had no idea, Sam."

"I didn't want to force my religion on you."

Alex glanced at the box on the table and fixed her eyes on the hole where the bullet had pierced the hands of Christ.

What if he was right? What if his life was saved by a divine power, and all he believes in is true? Sam had always been there for her, supporting her, carrying her through her disease. Given her hope and purpose. How could she deny him this?

She turned her eyes to his and found peace in his warm brown eyes.

"Let's do this."

CHAPTER 26

"Then it's settled," Matt said. "I'll man HQ while you two decipher and follow the text. I'll assemble the tactical team in the interim and meet you back here, hopefully with whatever's worth paying twenty million dollars for. Your trackers are live and we'll be able to stay in touch with these ear mics. They will automatically activate once you put them in your ear and transmit via satellite, hopefully even from below ground. I expect you to keep me in the loop at all times. I can't protect you if I don't know what's going on."

Matt handed them their earpieces.

"Testing, testing," he spoke into a receiver to which they responded.

Alex checked the cartridge of her weapon and placed the loaded gun in its usual spot. Sam did the same, slipping two more full clips into the pocket of his combat pants.

Satisfied they were protected as much as was within his means, Matt stepped back and placed his hands on his hips.

"Are you sure about this? It's not too late. I'm sure our advertiser will settle for the code on its own."

"We're sure. Sam and I have got this. Besides, it's what we do, isn't it? Protect and recover antiquities."

"Agreed. I can't think of anyone better equipped to handle this job anyway. Shall we tackle the cipher then?"

"Already done, mate. At least I know where we should kick off. It's the Temple Mount inside the Old City."

"Alex glanced sideways at Sam. You're sure?"

"Fairly, yes. I only know of one son of David and that was Solomon... King Solomon."

"What does he have to do with the Temple Mount? There's nothing but the Dome of the Rock on there. Are you saying it's inside the rock?" Matt asked.

"I doubt that," Alex answered on Sam's behalf. "The Dome of the Rock was built centuries after Caiaphas was alive. He couldn't have hidden anything in there."

"Exactly, but long before that, it was originally where they had built the Temple for Solomon, around 957 BC," Sam added.

"He's right. According to Britannica, The First Temple was built as an abode for the Ark and as a place of assembly for the entire people. Quote unquote," Ronita confirmed with her research.

"Then Nebuchadnezzar II destroyed it, which is incidentally when the Ark of the Covenant went missing, and it was only in 538 BC that Cyrus II, founder of the Achaemenian dynasty of Persia and conqueror of Babylonia rebuilt the Temple. The Temple treasure was plundered circa 54 BC after which the King of Judaea, Herod, rebuilt it again. It was then known as the Second Temple and construction took forty-six years to complete. It was during this time that Caiaphas was alive and it was where the Jewish people gathered to worship. The Second Temple was the very heartbeat of Jerusalem and not only used for religious ceremonies, but also as a repository for Holy Scriptures. The Sanhedrin, which was the Jewish high court which later oversaw Christ's hearing, gathered there too. It was only when the Muslim armies captured Jerusalem around AD 691, that they built the Dome as a monument, a symbol of power."

"So that's why the Muslims, Jews and Christians are fighting over it; their religions are all rooted in that one location," Alex surmised.

"Exactly, and to complicate it even further, it's also where the Knights Templar established themselves in 1119 and used the underground tunnels as their headquarters," Sam continued.

"And you think when you crack the Caiaphas code it will lead to whatever treasure they're after, even though there's no actual Temple structure to speak of anymore?" Matt asked.

"I do."

"So what do you think the code will lead us to? Caiaphas was certainly wealthy enough to have left some worthy loot," Matt continued.

"Perhaps he got his grubby little hands on the Temple Treasury," Ronita added her thoughts.

"We'll soon find out. But first we need to find a way into the underground tunnels. The place is crawling with security," Alex commented as she pored over the live feed of the security cameras Red had tapped into.

"I think I might be able to help with that," Ronita spoke. "There's apparently a network of tunnels underneath the Old City which was supposedly built by the Templars. Most of it's been destroyed but there's one area currently open to tourists. The entrance is through a section in the Wailing Wall. If you can sneak in before they shut the doors, you might find your way through the part that's been closed off to the public." Ronita handed a printed copy of the tunnel grid to Alex.

"There's no guarantee we'll be able to get to the rest of the tunnels from there but it certainly seems to be our best option."

"It's worth a shot. Great work, Ronnie. That's their way in. Time to crack on then, mates. This hunt has my curiosity piqued to the max." Matt let out a nervous giggle.

W ith the scheme carefully plotted Alex and Sam entered the Old City through the Dung Gate. With it being the closest access point to the Wailing Wall, Red had cleverly hacked the security system, which allowed them entry without their firearms getting detected. Camouflaged as tourists the pair vigilantly wandered around the Western Wall plaza.

"Seems clear," Sam commented to Alex after careful surveillance of their surrounds.

"Let's move in toward the wall," she suggested.

The plaza was, as was the case most of the time, crowded with tourists and religious followers. A small group of armed Israeli soldiers stood on guard outside a doorway positioned to one side of the Western Wall.

"That must be it," Alex noted when they drew nearer.

Simulating a happy couple taking photos, Sam used Alex as a decoy to zoom his camera's lens in on the tunnel entrance behind her.

"The coast is clear, we're going in," Sam reported to Matt via his ear mic.

"Copy that. Watch your backs though. Once you're inside we won't have cameras on you," Matt warned.

Entering the Western Wall tunnels went off without a glitch and Alex and Sam quickly found themselves descending the ancient stone staircase below the Old City walls. Partially lit for the benefit of the tourists, the main tunnel extended several yards to where it abruptly ended in a small area where four Jewish women stood facing the wall in prayer. Apart from their low murmured prayers, the small closed-off area was quiet. Alex turned in search of another tunnel but there was nothing there, nor did they pass any.

"It's a dead end, Sam. There's no access here to any other tunnels."

Sam studied Ronita's grid map.

"According to this, we're in the right place."

"This can't be the only tunnel, Sam. If this one exists there must be more."

Sam stared ahead.

"Then why the soldiers outside?"

"Protection maybe. There are always riots amongst the followers. Let's go back out and walk along the wall."

But searching for another entrance along the crowded Wailing Wall proved harder than anticipated. Rows of Jewish pilgrims lined the wall as they fervidly waited their turns to place a prayer into the cracks of the wall. And since Alex and Sam weren't permitted to walk too close to the wall, it made it even harder to spot any hidden openings. From the corner of her eye Alex glimpsed two suspicious looking men spying on them.

"Two possible threats at my nine o'clock," she reported to Matt through her earpiece.

"Copy that, Alex. We have eyes on them. I take it the tunnel was a dead end."

"Affirmative."

"Ronnie says there's something called the Foundation Stone that's accessible from within the Dome of the Rock. It leads to an underground chamber that was used for worship. The problem is it's entirely inaccessible to the public. You'd have to find a way to get inside the building undetected."

"Got it," Sam confirmed receipt of Matt's intel.

Alex's suspicions were indeed accurate when the two spies trailed them as they set off towards the entrance to the

Temple Mount upon which the Dome of the Rock was built. Picking up the pace while using the large number of visitors in their favor, Alex and Sam shook the men off their trail moments before they managed to slip in through the heavily guarded Temple Mount entrance. The renowned octagonal structure with its iconic gilded dome was majestic amidst the half dozen tourists that meandered the site around it. Positioned in front of the shrine, soldiers in pairs guarded each of its four entrances, which were entirely closed off to visitors, and nearly impossible to penetrate undetected.

"I hope Ronnie's intel is correct. This is going to take some doing," Sam commented as he and Alex walked the exterior in search of a way inside.

"We need a diversion. Something to distract the guards from one of the doors."

Alex stopped next to the nearby remnants of an ancient stone fountain where two soldiers guarded a door directly opposite while her mind conjured a way to distract them. Her eyes settled on the camera dangling from Sam's neck.

"Remove the camera's lens."

"Why, what brilliant idea has your brain concocted now?"

Alex ignored Sam's playful question. Instead she folded the tourist map she carried around in half before placing it on top of her headscarf on the edge of the fountain. She glanced up at the sun that cast blazing hot rays down onto them and placed the lens on top of the paper, angling the glass to have the rays beat down through it onto the paper with perfect precision.

"Now we wait," she whispered, and walked up to an open space on the wall to admire the renowned blue mosaic tiles on the building.

Her clever tactic paid off and it took hardly any time for the map to ignite and in turn spread through the cloth as it grew into a small fire. Startled by the unexpected fire that erupted in front of them, both guards rushed towards it, which provided the perfect distraction they needed to slip through the doors.

CHAPTER 27

"I cannot believe that worked!" Sam said as they closed the wooden doors behind them.

"Me neither, but I don't think we have a lot of time before they follow obvious protocol and search inside. Any idea what a Foundation Stone is?"

"Yes, it's a stone," Sam said with his usual dry humor.

"I would've never guessed that," she joked back.

The couple swiftly moved through the expansive open area in search of a stone-like object and soon came to a sudden halt above a large cordoned off, gaping hole in the earth on the far side of the building.

"Well, I would have never," Sam said as they stared down from the surrounding railing into the massive orange colored cavern in the floor. "How it translates to an underground tunnel system fails me but hey, Ronita's research proved sound so far."

Alex rushed towards the opening in the surrounding railing.

"If there's a hole in the ground there's a tunnel somewhere."

Fifteen stone steps led them down beneath the shrine's floor to where they arrived in a massive underground chamber where several prayer niches devoted to David and Solomon stared back at them.

"Alex, Sam, do you read me?" Matt's voice came through their earpieces.

"Loud and clear, mate. What's up?"

"We have a problem. Ravid just arrived and ordered the guards to stand down. He and his mob are about to gate-crash your party."

"How did he know we were here?" Alex asked, just as she heard one of the doors above ground squeak open.

"His goons have been on your tail since you entered the Old City. Somehow we missed them. Can you get out of there?"

"Negative," Alex whispered back.

Above their heads the squeaky sounds of shoes on the tile floors drew nearer. With their impending arrival Alex's heart settled into an uneven rhythm that had her eyes frantically searching for a way out. Apart from the gaping hole above their heads, the chamber was entirely closed all around them. They were trapped. Out of options and out of time, Alex and Sam ran toward the shaded area of one of the walls that appeared to offer the beginnings of another recess in the rock face that seemed to be under construction. As they silently moved across the poorly lit cavern floor, and their eyes adjusted to the darkness, the outline of a tunnel opening appeared from within the alcove. Without a second thought they ran into the underground passage moments before Ravid's men descended upon the railing that surrounded the Foundation Stone site above. Forced into the very pits of the Holy Land, blinded by total darkness, Alex and Sam ran towards the unknown. With a fair distance now between them and their pursuers, Alex finally switched on her flashlight and directed its beams into the tunnel ahead of them. Made entirely from limestone, the narrow subterranean passage with its dome-shaped ceiling had no end in sight and seemed to go on forever. Sam turned his attention to the entrance of the tunnel behind them, listening closely for evidence of Ravid and his men. Alerted only by the loose stones under the mob's feet in the tunnel behind them it was clear they were gaining ground.

"Let's hope we're not being chased into the jaws of a man-eating bull at the end of this passage. How far do you think this goes?" Sam said, as he ducked and narrowly missed a protruding brick from colliding with his head.

"Matt, we could do with a little help here," Alex pleaded over the microphone but Matt didn't answer.

She tried again but got the same result.

"We've lost comms with HQ." Sam stated the obvious. "Use that submarine gadget of yours and see if there's another way out."

"Unfortunately that gadget was on my phone and now no longer exists. We have no option but to keep running."

But just as all hope of reaching a way out had gone, Alex came to an abrupt stop when a slight breeze brushed her cheek.

"Wait!" she whispered to Sam and hurriedly took a step or two back. While she scanned her flashlight against the walls, her eyes caught the slightest crevice in the wall under the light of her torch.

"Feel that? There must be another tunnel behind this wall."

Alex pushed her palms against the stone wall and welcomed the sensation of it disappearing between the surrounding stones before it fell to the ground on the other side of the wall. Warmth spread through her body as she pushed several more strategic stone bricks and the crevice soon widened in the rock wall. With heightened enthusiasm they hurriedly created an opening in the wall, big enough for both of them to slip through. Adrenaline surged through their veins as Ravid and his men's footsteps grew louder by the second and in the midst of their euphoria, Alex and Sam gathered enough clarity to replace most of the bricks to cover their tracks. And not a moment too soon. Anxious not to make their presence known on the loose rocks under their feet, they remained in position, praying their hiding place would remain undetected. Barely breathing, enveloped by complete darkness, Alex and Sam pinned their bodies against their secret tunnel's wall, shutting their eyes in fear of being discovered. With their senses now in overdrive, Ravid and his men's feet shuffled past their secret hideout until Alex and Sam could no longer determine their position. Doubt flooded their minds as to whether or not the men had continued down the main underground passage or if they might have paused outside the barely visible opening. Standing nearest to the small gap in the wall, Alex opened her eyes and carefully searched for any signs of flashlights. Voices echoed back from further down the main tunnel, declaring that they had successfully escaped Ravid and his men's pursuit.

"They're gone," she whispered to Sam and flashed her torchlight into their newly discovered subterranean passage.

It looked much like the main one except that it was slightly narrower and not as well maintained. Neither spoke as they slowly made their way down the tunnel and much to their surprise, they soon reached another underground chamber. They stood frozen to the spot at the entrance while they shone their flashlights across the hollow space to take it all in. The ochre colored roof was dome shaped and rested upon nine column-like structures each separated by an alcove. Adorned with patterned carvings that mimicked the ones found on both rings and the box, it was clear they had discovered a chamber that might very well date back to the Second Temple period.

"What is this place?" Alex said.

Sam had left her side and honed his attention in on a particular carving in one of the recesses. It was a picture of a man praying next to an altar on top of which lay a young boy.

"It makes perfect sense now!" Sam exclaimed and yanked the code from his pocket.

"What does?"

"The cipher. *Look upon the son of David*. We know that refers to the Solomon Temple, which is this very site. Then it says *beneath the covenant of our Lord most high*. That part I haven't figured out yet but the next part *where the father of many sons sacrificed one, and the Almighty prophesied*. This is Abraham! Abraham was the father of many sons and many religious scholars believe the Temple

Mount is the very place where he came to sacrifice his son, Isaac."

"He sacrificed his son! As in through a burnt offering? That's awful!"

"No, no, he didn't have to. It was all just a test. God tested Abraham's faith and obedience to Him, which he passed with flying colors. God spared Isaac's life and he actually became the very person from whom Jesus descended, thus playing a pivotal role in the story of redemption. Look here, this image is of Abraham praying next to his son on the altar. That's the clue. We're exactly where the cipher says to look."

Sam's heart raced with excitement over his discovery. For the first time in all the years he'd been by Alex's side, he felt truly alive. He rushed between the alcoves in search of more etchings and stopped dead in his tracks as his eyes caught sight of parts of a faint image buried under a thin layer of sand. In his heart his mind had already conceived the rest of the image that lay hidden beneath the earth. With trembling hands he brushed the dry sandy powder from the rock wall to reveal an image of a chest-like box on top of which were two angels, whose large wings joined together to cover the entire body of the chest. Sam felt himself go weak at the knees as he shone his torch between the Caiaphas code in his hand and the image on the wall in front of him.

"It's the Ark of the Covenant," Alex spoke softly next to him.

"Beneath the covenant of our Lord most high," Sam read the cipher out loud.

Alex was first to shine her flashlight directly below the image and down the rock face onto the floor where she paused its light on top of one of the limestone squares in the floor in front of their feet. Feeling lightness in her chest she drew Sam's attention to the floor by gently nudging him with her elbow.

"Beneath the covenant of our Lord most high," she repeated.

As they knelt next to the stone, barely able to control the rapid thudding in their chests, their fingers brushed away the loose dirt that covered what neither expected to see.

CHAPTER 28

E motions gripped their very core when their fingers traced the carved lines of precise replicas of the two Caiaphas rings' seals, spaced about seven inches apart. Words eluded the elated pair as Sam reached into his pocket and pulled out the two rings. They were a perfect match.

"This is it, Sam. We've deciphered the Caiaphas code."

A broad smile flashed across his face.

"There's only one thing left to do then." Sam handed one of the rings to Alex.

"Ready?" he whispered.

With unsteady hands they turned their respective rings over and placed the seals into each of the carved images in the stone. The faintest series of clicks, mimicking those of the cogs and springs of a watch, sounded from beneath the stone before the stone gently lifted away at each of its sides. Sam lifted the square slab from the floor as Alex beamed her flashlight down into the cavity. There, buried deep in the foundations of Israel's Holy City, Alex and Sam recovered a smaller replica of the ancient reliquary they had found the coded text in mere days before.

"Do you think it's another code?" Sam asked as he lifted the box from the ground and held it under Alex's flashlight.

"There's only one way of finding out, isn't there? Open it."

Under the strong beam of Alex's torch, a small purple velvet pouch came into vision. Threaded together at the opening by a gold silk string, Alex lifted it out and gently slid the gathering over the delicate cord. She tipped the somewhat weighty contents of the pouch into Sam's hand and he drew in a sharp breath the instant his mind determined what lay in his palms. Overwhelmed by emotion, Sam fought to hold back his tears.

Confused by her husband's sudden uncharacteristic emotional state, Alex placed her hand on Sam's arm.

"What's happening? What is it?"

Sam wiped his cheek where a lonely tear rolled down onto his chin and stared into his wife's confused eyes.

"If I'm right, and I think I am, then I'm holding the three nails that were used to crucify Jesus Christ."

Alex stared down at the three iron spikes with their tips hammered to one side. Almost perfectly preserved with traces of what might be blood, it was clear the iron nails were handmade and not manufactured by modern machinery.

"Do you know what this means, Alex? These, along with the original biblical scriptures that have already been found, prove Christ's existence, His crucifixion and the very foundation of Christianity. Caiaphas buried these in offering to God, here beneath where I believe the Ark of the Covenant was once hidden, seeking God's forgiveness for plotting Christ's death. *With this my atonement unto Thee, in the hope to forever be set free.* That's the final part of the code."

Alex took a moment to digest his statement. She believed him. But as her mind returned to its fully rational state as the initial adrenalin wore off, she opened the purple pouch and held it out to Sam to collect the nails.

"We need to get out of here. There's a twenty-million-dollar bounty out for these. And if these are what you say they are, we have to prevent whoever's behind the darknet touting from getting his hands on it."

Sobered by Alex's sensible words, Sam agreed and it wasn't long before they replaced the slab in the floor and made off with the box and its contents towards the main tunnel.

The secret tunnel's exit was exactly as they had left it. Alert and with caution they listened out for Ravid and his men. When they were satisfied there was no one on the other side of the previously deconstructed wall, they quietly removed each stone and proceeded with caution along the main underground tunnel. Apart from their footsteps sounding lightly on the stone floor, it was completely quiet.

"They must have left through an exit at the other end of this tunnel," Sam whispered when they neared the Foundation Stone chamber and there was still no sign of danger.

But Alex wasn't so sure. It almost seemed too quiet. She reached back and pulled her firearm from its place in the small of her back. Something wasn't right. She sensed it. Sam saw that Alex was clearly not convinced they were safe and readied his gun also before he followed her with vigilance. Ten feet ahead of them the dim light from the chamber alerted them that they had reached the end of the tunnel. Alex paused, flexing her fingers over her gun's grip and stretched it out in front of her. With stealth they approached and exited into the chamber. Sudden movement, instantly followed by the simultaneous cocking of rifles, echoed above their heads. Jolted into submission under the aim of Ravid and five of his rogue soldiers, Alex and Sam contemplated the dire situation they now found themselves in.

"I knew you'd eventually surface. Drop your guns," Ravid ordered from the railing above their heads.

Alex steadied her legs in a defense position and gripped her gun tighter while she aimed it directly at Ravid.

"You are surrounded. There's no way out of this alive, Alex Hunt. Now put your weapons down and slowly make your way to the steps."

Compelled to do as he instructed, Alex and Sam reluctantly surrendered and dropped their guns on the floor. With their hands in the air they slowly made their way to the bottom of the steps as ordered.

"Good, now slowly take the loot out and put it down on the stairs, then go back."

Alex threw a sideways glance at Sam as she realized Ravid had no idea what the Caiaphas code had led them to. She hoped Sam discerned that too. Since she was unable to divulge an impromptu strategy to Sam, she concentrated her mind on the plan in the hope their telepathic communication system would work. Alex bit at the inside of her cheek and remained in place. There was no guarantee Sam would've caught on and no way she would find out either.

"I don't know what you're talking about," she bluffed in an attempt to glean more information on precisely how much Ravid really knew.

"The code, Alex. I assume you must have discovered the scroll that contains some sort of cipher. Hand it over."

Ravid's last declaration was precisely the information she had hoped to extract, and with his hand now played, Sam in turn knew too.

"Fine, put your weapons down and I'll give it to you," Sam joined the negotiations.

"That's not going to happen, Dr. Quinn, and now that you've just confirmed you have it I have no reason to keep you alive."

Ravid pushed his chin out as a signal to one of his men to kill them. Alex felt her back stiffen in anticipation of being shot.

"That will only get you half of the bounty, Ravid. We can decipher the code and you can walk off with another ten million," Alex shouted at him.

Ravid commanded his man to stand down. The look on his face told them he'd had no idea there was more money in play.

"Oh, you didn't know that did you?" Sam declared.

Ravid's face flushed red with embarrassment over getting trumped.

"Let Sam go and I'll tell you where it is."

Alex's words blew a hole through Sam's gut.

"What are you doing?" Sam snapped at Alex.

She ignored him.

"Well isn't that cute. But spare me the romantic gestures. I'm not letting either one of you go. You have exactly three seconds to tell me where the treasure is or I'll kill you both and figure it out myself."

There was no way to recover from their poor odds so Alex agreed.

"Fine, it's out there, near the fountain." Alex nudged her head toward the Dome of the Rock's exit.

Ravid instructed two of his men to apprehend Alex and Sam and watched his men escort them up the steps. Held captive by their rifles that pushed firmly onto their spines, Alex and Sam led Ravid and his men towards one of the shrine's exit doors. From somewhere behind them the unexpected explosion of rapid gunfire caught them all off guard. Using it to their advantage Alex and Sam bolted toward the door and narrowly escaped the bullets from an unknown person who had somehow managed to gun down Ravid and all of his men.

Alex and Sam ran across Temple Mount. Tourists and pilgrims scattered off in all directions. Unarmed and unable to fire back they had no option but to take cover behind a nearby stone structure when another onslaught of bullets whistled past their heads.

"These aren't bounty hunters, Alex," Sam observed as they waited for another opportunity to escape their attackers, who were closing in fast.

"They're not!" Matt's voice suddenly came through their earpieces. "We managed to flush them out from the underbelly of the Dark Web. Sit tight, help is on the way."

But whilst Matt's voice and promise of help provided some relief, Alex and Sam were still very much in danger.

"We've got to get out of here, Sam," Alex barely managed to get out as several more bullets hit the stone structure behind them. With their hiding place clearly compromised, they had no idea how many attackers there were or where they were positioned. If they tried to escape they would certainly get killed.

"Hold your fire! I need them alive!" An unfamiliar male voice resounded through the air.

His American accent left both Alex and Sam dazed with confusion where they remained hidden behind the stone structure.

"You're about to become very rich, whoever you are!" the American shouted out toward them. "Come out so we can talk. I won't hurt you; I just want to talk."

"Matt, tell your men to approach quietly. We're about to build an airtight case for you, mate," Sam spoke into his mic.

"Copy that."

Another invitation to come out of hiding had Alex and Sam on their feet with their hands raised in the air. Across from them a tall, middle-aged man stood between half a dozen armed civilians. His raven black hair, offset by a crisp, white cotton shirt and equally casual linen pants, curled loosely over his ears and against his neck. Looking like he might have just stepped off a luxury yacht in the south of France, he approached them, dangling a pair of expensive tortoiseshell sunglasses between his fingers.

"Allow me to introduce myself. I'm Daniel Levine. What you have in your possession is worth a lot to me and I'm prepared to reward you handsomely for it. I'm assuming you found my humble invitation to earn enough to set you up for the rest of your life the same way the others did, so let's get the transaction done so we can all get on with our lives."

"How do we know you're good for the money?" Alex played along.

Her question evoked an arrogant smirk on Daniel Levine's tanned face. He summoned one of his men who opened an aluminum briefcase to display tightly packed parcels of hundred-dollar bills.

"This is one million dollars. There are nine more like this in my car just outside the City's walls and, assuming you've successfully deciphered the code, ten million more in a Swiss bank account ready to be transferred into your name. I don't play around when it comes to religious relics. Especially ones my family has fought to find for nearly fifty years. Now, do we have a deal?"

Alex and Sam didn't hesitate. Matt had already confirmed the tactical team was in place and ready to move in the moment they took receipt of the money.

"You have a deal," Sam said.

"Now, if you'd be so kind as to prove you have it, we can complete the transaction outside."

Sam retrieved the scroll from the zip pouch in his backpack and unrolled it for Daniel to inspect. His face lit up at the sight of the ancient coded scroll.

"And the nails?"

Again Sam reached inside his backpack and pulled out the small metal box, opening the pouch to reveal the three holy nails.

"Not so fast, Levine," Sam warned when he reached out to touch the relics.

"Of course, follow me."

With the scroll and the nails safely stowed inside Sam's bag, the pair followed the American and his posse to where a white Range Rover stood waiting just outside the Old City.

"It's all there," he said when his driver opened the trunk to reveal the nine other suitcases. He motioned to one of his men who had a laptop and moments later evidence of a Swiss bank account that displayed a balance of ten million dollars flashed across the screen.

Sam handed the scroll over and Alex took the first briefcase from Daniel Levine's hands.

"Get down on your knees!" The warning call came as a fully armed tactical team, led by Matt, descended on them and took the men down.

The unsuspecting announcement had Daniel react instantly by locking Alex into a firm grip from behind. With his back to his car, using it as a shield, he pushed his handgun against her temple.

"Back off or she's dead!"

"Don't be stupid, mate. You're surrounded. There's no way this is going to end well for you. Let her go."

Matt's words had the American in a panic, but he wasn't about to give up. With his forearm tightly gripped around Alex's neck and the gun firmly on her temple, he moved backwards around the side of the car toward the driver's door. Unaware of a tactical member that stood ready and waiting in anticipation of his ill-planned escape, the sudden awareness of his presence had Daniel aim his gun at him instead. Out from under his aim, Alex executed a defense tactic that freed her from his grip and had him pinned down by the tactical team in less than three seconds.

But not before he managed to fire off a single bullet that left Alex slumped to the ground.

CHAPTER 29

"There she is," Matt's jovial voice rang in her ears as Alex came to. "You took quite a punch there, Sheila."

Alex groaned as her hand moved towards her breastbone where the bullet's impact on the armored vest had left a substantial bruise. Aware she lay on top of an ambulance gurney next to the Range Rover, she turned to meet Sam's reassuring smile.

"Welcome back. You're fine. That was an insanely stupid move you pulled there that could've had you killed though."

"As long as you got Levine."

Matt threw his hands in the air. "Oh we got the guy, and some. Daniel Levine's been on the suspicious list for years and no one's ever been able to come close to catching the slimeball. One of Michigan City's most prominent art dealers. He and his family have been profiting from illegal trafficking rings all over the Middle East for almost fifty years. The guy has quite the little black book on his payroll too, anyone from dirty politicians to supreme court judges. He's eluded the US Art Crimes unit for decades. But now we've caught him red-handed on international soil so he stands no chance of getting out of this one. Thanks to Sam's voice recordings on his mobile and the surveillance camera footage, we've got a solid case that's going to put him behind bars for years."

Matt excused himself when one of the tactical team's agents pulled him aside.

"What about the Caiaphas Code and the holy nails?" Alex asked Sam with concern.

"They're being handed to the Israeli Archaeology Association as we speak. As it turns out, the crucifixion nails were the final items needed to complete what Levine calls his Trinity collection. Somehow he'd already obtained the Shroud of Turin and the Crown of Thorns, all of which will be moved to the Byzantine and Christian Museum in Athens."

"That's quite the collection." Alex fell silent as she swung her legs over the side of the gurney and stared at the ground.

"Why the long face? I thought you'd be over the moon about it," Sam commented.

"I am, honestly. It's just that... well... I'm going to miss this."

"Miss this. What are you talking about?"

Alex took Sam's hand in hers and gently placed it on her belly.

"I'm pregnant."

> *"Now faith is the substance of things hoped for,*
> *the evidence of things not seen."*
> *Hebrews 11:1*

BEHIND THE CAIAPHAS CODE

DOWNLOAD the exclusive BEHIND THE CAIAPHAS CODE booklet **FREE! Crammed with my research links, additional information and an exclusive inside view of the characters in my head!**

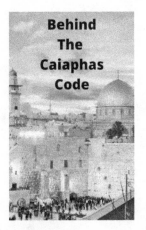

Not available anywhere else

AUTHOR CONNECT

No-Spam Newsletter
ELITE SQUAD

FOLLOW Urcelia Teixeira

BookBub has a New Release Alert. Not only can you check out the latest deals, but you can also get an email when I release my next book by following me here

https://www.bookbub.com/authors/urcelia-teixeira

Website:
https://www.urcelia.com

Facebook:
https://www.facebook.com/urceliabooks

Twitter:
https//www.twitter.com/UrceliaTeixeira

ALEX HUNT Adventure Thrillers

Also suited as standalone novels

The **PAPUA INCIDENT - Prequel (sign up to get it FREE)**

The **RHAPTA KEY**

The **GILDED TREASON**

The **ALPHA STRAIN**

The **DAUPHIN DECEPTION**

The **BARI BONES**

The **CAIAPHAS CODE**

ABOUT THE AUTHOR

Urcelia Teixeira is an author of fast-paced archaeological action-adventure novels with a Christian nuance.

Readers have described her Alex Hunt Adventure Thriller Series as 'Indiana Jones meets Lara Croft with a twist of Bourne.' She read her first book when she was four and wrote her first poem when she was seven. And though she lived vicariously through books, and her far too few travels, life happened. She married the man of her dreams and birthed three boys (and added two dogs, a cat, three chickens, and some goldfish!) So, life became all about settling down and providing a means to an end. She climbed the corporate ladder, exercised her entrepreneurial flair and made her mark in real estate.

Traveling and exploring the world made space for child-friendly annual family holidays by the sea. The kind where she succumbed to building sandcastles and barely got past reading the first five pages of a book. And on the odd occasion she managed to read fast enough to reach page eight, she was confronted with a moral dilemma as the umpteenth expletive forced its way off just about every page!

But by divine intervention, upon her return from yet another male-dominated camping trip, when fifty knocked hard and fast on her door, and she could no longer stomach the profanities in her reading material, she drew a line in the sand and bravely set off to create a new adventure!

It was in the dark, quiet whispers of the night, well past midnight late in the year 2017, that Alex Hunt was born.

Her philosophy

From her pen, flow action-packed adventures for the armchair traveler who enjoys a thrilling escape. Devoid of the usual profanity and obscenities, she incorporates real-life historical relics and mysteries from exciting places all over the world. She aims to kidnap her reader from the mundane and plunge them into feel-good riddle-solving quests filled with danger, sabotage, and mystery!

For more visit www.urcelia.com or email her on books@urcelia.com

facebook.com/urceliateixeira

twitter.com/urcelia_teixeira

instagram.com/urceliateixeira

PRAYER OF SALVATION

If you've read this book along with all the supporting research in the Bonus download, and feel that God is calling your name, then take a private moment and say this prayer.

"Dear God, I am a sinner and need your forgiveness. I believe that Jesus Christ shed His precious blood and died for my sins. I am willing to change and turn from my sins. I now invite Jesus Christ to come into my heart and life as my personal Savior."

Steps after this prayer
1. Believe you have been forgiven and accepted by God
2. Join a local Christian church and tell one of the staff on duty

3. Download a FREE digital copy of the Holy Bible and start reading Matthew, Mark, Luke and John

Paperback © ISBN: 978-0-6398434-3-8

Independently Published by Urcelia Teixeira

www.urcelia.com

books@urcelia.com

CPSIA information can be obtained
at www.ICGtesting.com
Printed in the USA
BVHW031946080920
588383BV00001B/108